COUNTER-ATTACK

Also by Leo Kessler

THE IRON FIST
THE TRAITORS
WOLF

In the *Wotan/Panzer* Series

SS PANZER BATTALION
DEATH'S HEAD
CLAWS OF STEEL
GUNS AT CASSINO
THE DEVIL'S SHIELD
HAMMER OF THE GODS
FORCED MARCH
BLOOD AND ICE
THE SAND PANTHERS

In the *Black Cossacks* Series

THE BLACK COSSACKS
THE BLACK COSSACKS 2: SABRES OF THE REICH
THE BLACK COSSACKS 3: MOUNTAIN OF SKULLS

In the *Stormtroop* Series

STORMTROOP
BLOOD MOUNTAIN

Leo Kessler

Counter-Attack

Futura Publications Limited
A Futura Book

A Futura Book

First published in Great Britain by
Futura Publications Limited in 1978

ISBN 0 7088 1349 6

Printed in Great Britain by
Hazell Watson & Viney Ltd
Aylesbury, Bucks

Futura Publications Limited
110 Warner Road
Camberwell, London SE5

'Soldiers of Battle Group Wotan! Germans! Comrades! To-night we return to the Reich. Tomorrow we begin to train a new Wotan. Already the barracks are filling with our new recruits – the cream of the Hitler Youth, young and idealistic, volunteers to the man. You and I will train them in the glorious, heroic battle-tradition of our formation, for which so many brave men have died. But the new Wotan will be different from the old one. It will be our regiment, an elite regiment run by us and for us. When we return to Berlin each and every one of you will become an NCO – my NCOs – All of you have fought and bled at my side. I know you all like a brother – you know me in the same way.*

We are comrades . . .

Repeat after me . . . in the name of the Führer, in the name of the Third Reich, and in the name of Wotan. I swear that I shall fight to the death . . . to keep our enemies from the Fatherland . . . And if I betray this oath, I shall be executed as a traitor to my Fatherland, my Führer and my comrades – and the Wotan!'

Col v. Dodenburg, C.O. SS Assault Regt. Wotan, Italy June 6th, 1944.[1]

---

[1] See *Guns at Cassino* for further details (transl.).

PRELUDE TO BATTLE

'Wotan is the most infamous SS regiment in the whole of the Wehrmacht. It has spearheaded every Jerry attack since 1939 . . . It has fought on every front and been decimated time and time again. But the old cadre of experienced officers and NCOs has always managed to lick it back into top shape again and there's never been a shortage of fanatical young Nazis to fill its ranks. They seem to consider it almost an honour to die for Wotan.'

Wing-Commander Winterbotham, British Intelligence,
to U.S. Gen. Bradley, 3 August, 1944

The tall blond Englishman in R.A.F. battledress hit the brakes. Hard. The camouflaged jeep slithered to a stop in a thick cloud of dust. *There* was the hole in the six-foot Norman hedgerow that they had told him about, further up the coastal road! He had arrived at his destination. He swung out of the driving seat, and lifting up the jeep's hood, began to take off the rotor arm.

Behind him on the road, trucks and jeeps carrying ammunition for the new break-out bumped and skidded along the shell-pitted road. To his right, sweating engineers in their undershirts were scraping out with their bulldozers a runway for a landing strip, while in the field beyond, coloured GIs of the Graves Registration Corps were burying the new dead of Patton's Third Army. There was an air of orderly, energetic confusion about the scene under the burning August sky which reminded the Englishman of the times in his youth when he had watched a circus being erected in the fields of his native Gloucestershire.

His jeep immobilized as regulations demanded, the Englishman crawled through the thick hedge of the *bocage*.

From now onwards it was footslogging only. Hastily he climbed the muddy bank beyond and clambered onto the path which led to the headquarters. Aware of the importance of his information, he jog-trotted across the lush green meadow, tired as he was from the long journey across the Channel. He ducked and crawled through another hedge to emerge into another world.

Ranged in a semi-circle around the leaward edge of a small orchard was the caravanserai of the 12th U.S. Army's HQ. To the Englishman it looked for all the world like a peacetime holiday-camp in some forgotten corner of Devon. Only the steady thud-thud of the heavies at the front were a reminder that a mere dozen miles away General Bradley's troops were fighting desperately to breach the German line after being trapped in the murderous *bocage* country ever since D-Day, two long months before.

A sentry barred the Englishman's way suddenly. The Englishman flashed his special pass. The GI had been at the HQ long enough to know that anyone with that kind of pass gained immediate admittance to the Commanding General. 'This way, *sir!*' he breathed, as if he had just bumped into God himself.

One minute later, the Englishman was facing the Commanding General in the office of his outsize caravan. General Omar Nelson Bradley shook his hand warmly, his eyes twinkling behind the steel-framed GI eyeglasses. 'Good to see you again, Winterbotham,' he said in that plaintive mid-Western accent of his. 'You boys in London have been a real help. I never expected to get such concise information about the other fellow. The only trouble is that there seem to be too many of the s.o.b.'s.' He grinned and offered the S.I.S. agent a seat.[1] 'And what brings you from the fleshpots of London to this particular neck of the woods?'

Group-Captain Winterbotham, the guardian of the pre-

[1] Secret Intelligence Service, i.e., British secret service.

cious Ultra[1] secret, flashed a glance at the door to the office. It was closed. He hesitated only a fraction of a second before plunging into the reason for his hasty journey from London to war-torn Normandy.

'General, yesterday we cracked a signal from Hitler's HQ to the new Commander-in-Chief in the West, Field Marshal von Kluge. The Jerries are beginning to move their armour from Monty's front – all of it.'

Bradley shot him a keen glance, his heavy-jawed face suddenly hard and set. 'Who they gonna hit?' he demanded.

'*You!*'

'Brother!' Bradley exclaimed. 'All right, Winterbotham, give it to me – straight on the chin.'

'It was a two-paged signal, sir. Hitler ordered von Kluge to pull out all the SS armour on Monty's front, plus whatever else he could scrape together in the way of tanks, and some five infantry divisions. Their aim is to recapture Avranches and —'

'You don't need to paint me a picture, Winterbotham,' Bradley interrupted. 'That crazy Patton is already rampaging deep into Brittany. If the other fellow can break through to the sea at Avranches, he would cut off Patton's nine divisions in Brittany and at the same time he would trap the remainder of 12th Army's troops back in the difficult *bocage* countryside from which it has taken us nearly eight weeks to break out.'

'Exactly, sir.'

Bradley stroked his heavy, pugnacious jaw. 'All right, where – and when?'

'According to the signal, Hitler has ordered his élite unit SS Assault Regiment Wotan to lead the attack. It will strike at the small town of Mortain at dawn on August 7th.'

'So I've got two days to get ready for them, eh?' Bradley mused, while the tall Englishman watched the American

[1] The top secret organization which was able to decipher *all* the German signals transmitted by means of the German Enigma coding machine between topmost enemy commands, including those of Hitler himself.

carefully for any sign of weakness or fear. But the prospect that his thin flank was going to be hit by a total of nine divisions did not seem to worry the General. His face remained thoughtful but unalarmed.

'But I must remind you, sir, that *on no account* must the forward American troops be alerted to the impending attack by the Jerries. The Prime Minister was explicit on that. It would compromise Ultra seriously if the Jerries felt they had walked into a trap. In a situation like that they could well conclude that the whole plan of the attack had been given away by their own signals, and that would be the end of Ultra. They'd probably change their whole system.'

Bradley nodded his head slowly. 'I see. You can assure Winnie[1] that the leading troops won't be alerted. Though of course I shall have to move in fresh troops to take the blow once the attack has really started.'

'Agreed, sir. The Prime Minister has no objections to that. But on the first day of the attack your men must manage the best they can against the Wotan.'

Bradley scratched his shaven head. 'Wotan. Haven't I heard the name of that outfit before, Winterbotham?'

'I'd be surprised if you hadn't, sir. Wotan is the most infamous SS regiment in the whole of the *Wehrmacht*. It has spearheaded every Jerry attack since 1939 – Belgium, Holland, France, Greece, Africa, Russia – it's fought on every front and been decimated time and time again. But the old cadre of experienced officers and NCOs has always managed to lick it back into top shape again and there's never been a shortage of fanatical young Nazis to fill its ranks. They seem to consider it almost an honour to die for Wotan. In short, sir, SS Assault Regiment Wotan is the toughest unit the Germans have. The "Führer's Fire-Brigade" they call it on the other side of the line.'

'And I'm supposed to let a bunch of killers like that loose on my unsuspecting doughs holding the left flank?' Bradley queried, his eyes suddenly very worried.

[1] Nickname for the British Prime Minister, Winston Churchill.

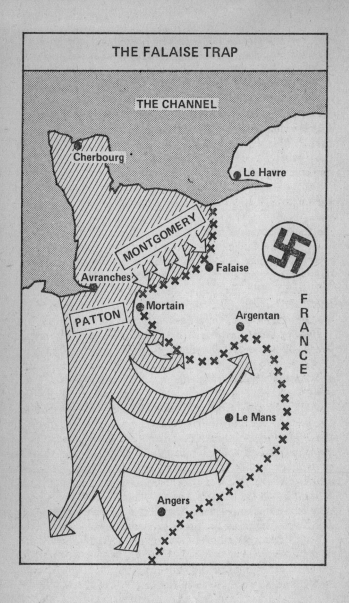

THE FALAISE TRAP

THE CHANNEL

Cherbourg

Le Havre

MONTGOMERY

Falaise

Avranches

PATTON

Mortain

Argentan

F
R
A
N
C
E

Le Mans

Angers

Winterbotham nodded his head slowly. 'If we want to keep the secret of Ultra, sir,' he said, 'I'm afraid you will be forced to. There is no other way.'

General Bradley looked out of the caravan's window. Outside, the August sky looked leaden and ominous. 'My poor doughs,' he said softly, almost as if he were talking to himself, 'my poor bloody doughs . . .'

ATTACK!

'Believe you me, ape-turd, before this month is out, a lot of those lucky lads are gonna be looking at the taties from beneath.'

Sgt-Major Schulze to Corporal Matz, Aug 6th, 1944

ONE

'Hey, carrot-cock.'

Corporal Matz of SS Assault Regiment Wotan, who was standing completely naked in the August sunshine, looked up from the task of powdering the inflamed stump of his right leg and stared across at the giant frame of Sergeant-Major Schulze. 'You talking to me, currant-crapper?'

With great deliberation, the big ex-docker from Hamburg's waterfront continued to clean his blackened toenails with the point of his bayonet. 'No, I thought you was Field Marshal shitting von Kluge,' he said, without rancour, artistically nicking out a particularly obstinate piece of dirt from behind his big toenail.

Matz broke wind noisily.

'Heil Hitler!' Schulze said routinely. 'But what I was going to say,' he continued, 'is that – did you know that the average Frog slit never wears drawers, 'cept to go to the synagogue on Sundays?'

'Very handy,' Matz commented, dabbing more powder on the sore stump, the result of nearly a month of fighting at Caen against the Tommies without being able to take his dice-beakers off. 'So, pea-pisser, what does that mighty brain of yours conclude from that fact?'

'That the Frogs can whip it in, whip it out and wipe it off, just like that.' He clicked his thumb and forefinger

13

together noisily. 'Consequently the decadent swine are allus worn out, so that they don't have time to go to war and have their stupid great turnips shot off like us Aryan, Greater German, pricks. That's what I conclude, you one-legged crippled pea-shitter.' With his free hand he reached for the looted bottle of Calvados and swigged the French apple brandy greedily.

Matz's little brown eyes followed the rapidly descending level of the fiery spirit anxiously. 'Watch that schnapps, sauce-snout,' he rapped. 'There are other blokes around, you know.'

'Like who, arse with ears?' Schulze grunted, wiping his unshaven chin free of liquid with the back of his massive paw. He tossed the bottle to his running-mate, who caught it with a practised hand. 'Here you are. Give your syphilitic tonsils a treat.'

'*Merci*,' Matz said, and lost no time in belting down a mighty slug of their last bottle of booze. 'You think we're in for it again, Schulzi?' he queried, when he had finished.

'Sure,' his companion replied easily. 'Any time now the shit's gonna hit the fan.'

'What makes you think so?'

'Gimme a lung torpedo and I'll put yer in the big picture, you garden dwarf.'

'All right, Rembrandt, put me in the picture.' Matz took the half-smoked cigarette from behind his ear and tossed it to the giant.

Schulze caught it neatly and with a quick gesture of his thumb-nail lit a match. He puffed out a cloud of contented blue smoke. 'It's as plain as a prick on a bush nigger,' he said. 'All last month we've been banging away at those buck-toothed Tommies and got nowhere – fast. Now Wotan has been moved down here to the other end of the front and you can bet your last mark that we're not here to have a little rest cure. We're gonna have a bash at the Amis.'

'Well, I'll piss up my sleeve!' Matz exclaimed. 'I thought

the Greatest Captain of All Times[1] was gonna give us a little break.'

'Slide down my back, corkscrew-cock,' Schulze said contemptuously. 'When did Adolf ever worry about the SS's welfare? We're expendable, mate. You've been with this mob nearly five years now. Even a bird-brain like you should know that. It's allus been march or croak for SS Assault Regiment Wotan.' With an expansive gesture, he swept his big paw of a hand around at the young, smooth-cheeked boys, in their black uniforms with the shining silver SS runes at the collar, who sprawled in the long summer grass beside the camouflaged Panthers and Tigers, enjoying this time out of war. 'Believe you me, ape-turd, before this month is out, a lot of those lucky lads are gonna be looking at the taties from beneath. Now get yer greedy little paws off'n that bottle of sauce and pass it back to Daddy . . .'

As usual, Sergeant-Major Schulze was right. For already, at that moment, the staff cars of the various commanders of the Corps to which SS Regiment Wotan belonged were arriving at the farmhouse HQ of SS Colonel-General Paul Hausser, who had overall command of the new counter-attack.

Skilfully, Colonel von Dodenburg, CO of the Wotan, steered his VW jeep by a group of captured GIs, white-faced and terrified, who were being hurried at the point of a bayonet to the HQ for interrogation by an ugly-faced private of the Armed SS. By the looks on their young faces, the handsome young Colonel with the keen blue eyes could tell that they already thought they were going to be put against the nearest wall and shot out of hand.

'Keep smiling, boys,' he said cheerfully in English, and braked to a stop next to a line of battered ambulances, their Red Cross markings peppered with machine-gun fire. There was no response from the frightened prisoners. Von Dodenburg shrugged, and pulling his black leather jacket, adorned solely by the black-and-white medal of the Knight's

[1] Contemptuous SS name for Adolf Hitler.

15

Cross of the Iron Cross, to cover the shrapnel holes in his black tank trousers, he stepped inside the HQ.

They were all waiting for him there – fat, be-monocled von Luttwitz of the 2nd Panzer; haughty, stupid Lamm-derding of the 2nd SS; cunning old Fritz Bayerlein of the *Panzerlehr*;[1] Count von Schwerin of the 116th, already a marked man because of his role in the recent plot to kill Hitler; and old Papa Hauser himself, one of the founders of the Armed SS, his lean face covered with old battle scars, a black eye-patch covering the socket of the eye he had lost at Moscow nearly three years before.

'Ay, the blue-eyed boy of Wotan at last,' von Luttwitz remarked in that supercilious manner of his. 'We *are* being honoured today!'

Hausser shot the *Wehrmacht* commander a hard look, but said nothing. Von Luttwitz was too good a tank commander to be fired just because he couldn't stand the Armed SS. Instead, he acknowledged von Dodenburg's salute and apology for being late, saying, 'All right, gentlemen, then shall we get down to cases?'

There was a murmur of agreement, and the commanders concentrated on the briefing, the animosities between the Armed SS generals and those of the regular *Wehrmacht* forgotten for a while.

'Gentlemen,' Hausser commenced, 'the Führer has ordered the execution of a break-through to the coast, in order to create the basis for a decisive operation against the Allied invasion front.'

Hastily he held up his hands to stop the sudden hum of interest. 'As the Führer has explained to Field Marshal von Kluge,' he went on, 'the successful execution of this operation will determine the decision of the war in the West, and with it perhaps the decision of the war itself.'

This time the one-eyed Colonel-General paused and let them think about his words. Outside there was the sharp burst of machine-pistol fire and the cries of the dying Americans. Von Dodenburg frowned. Why did the younger

[1] Demonstration Tank Division.

SS commanders let their fanatical troopers get away with murders like that, he asked himself. The Armed SS's reputation on the battlefield was frightening enough. Why did they allow themselves to be stamped as cold-blooded murderers who slaughtered their prisoners, too?

Before he had found an answer to that overwhelming question, Hausser continued his briefing. 'Commanders of all ranks must be absolutely clear as to the enormous significance of this operation, *meine Herren*. Absolutely! I expect all corps and divisional commanders to ensure that all subordinate officers, down to the company level, are aware of the unique significance of the whole situation. Clear?'

There was a murmur of agreement.

'Now, gentlemen, down to details.' Hausser turned and tapped the big situation map pinned up on the farmhouse wall behind him, just under the dusty crucifix which looked so strangely out of place in the HQ. 'Avranches, the hinge that has opened the door to Brittany through which that crazy cowboy general of theirs, Patton, is presently pouring division after division. Grab that hinge and we can close the door, leaving General Patton and his luckless soldiers stranded high and dry in the peninsula, cut off from their rear. Now, from our present positions along the line of Vire–Dove, we are about twenty kilometres from Avranches.' Hausser's single eye glittered. 'Think of it, gentlemen, twenty small kilometres from that single road and single bridge which link some three hundred thousand Amis with their rear! What a glittering prize!'

'Yes, indeed,' von Luttwitz boomed, screwing his monocle more firmly in his eye. 'And pray, how are we supposed to win that particular flower-pot?'

Hausser's thin craggy face flushed. 'I shall explain that in a moment, General,' he said stiffly. 'Now, the line-up for the attack is as follows – your 116th Panzer, von Schwerin, and your 2nd Panzer in the north, the 1st and 2nd SS in the centre, with your *Panzerlehr*, Bayerlein, and the remnants of the 5th SS Panzer Grenadier Division in the south.'

17

The assembled generals nodded their understanding, all save von Luttwitz, whose face betrayed cynical disbelief.

Hausser breathed out hard, like a man who bore many burdens. 'Now we all understand General von Luttwitz's point. How are we to advance, when the Allies have complete control of the sky above us?'

'That you can say again,' Bayerlein broke in, a grin on his good-humoured face. 'I don't think a day has passed in the last month when some damned Allied *Jabo*[1] or other hasn't made me cream my skivvies.'

There was a rumble of laughter from the generals, in which von Dodenburg joined. Fritz Bayerlein was at least a fighting general, who was always up at the Front with his tankers. Not like some of those present. For them, war was a series of plans, worked out in some HQ, remote from the dangers of the battlefield, based on training schools and textbooks, which they and their opponents had all read. If Plan A failed, then Plan B was put into operation, and if that failed too, then Plan C. For such commanders, war was like some great lethal game of chess, in which the pawns were irreplaceable young men. They never saw the vomit and the blood, they never heard the cries of the dying and the heartrending pleas of the wounded; for they fought their war in the antiseptic, clinical atmosphere of the rear HQ, with guards of honour at the door and wine for dinner, and if they were lucky, some nubile 'field mouse'[2] to spend the night with at the end of a hard day.

Von Dodenburg jerked his mind away from his thoughts and concentrated on Hausser's briefing. 'So how do we overcome the Allied advantage in the air?' Hausser was saying.

'Send in the *Luftwaffe*,' von Luttwitz suggested. 'Though I suppose the gentlemen flyboys are too busy expending their surplus energy in Paris to bother about the fate of a lot of poor stubble-hoppers like ourselves.'

Hausser ignored the comment. 'There is only one way

[1] Fighter-bomber.
[2] Nickname for the German Army female auxiliary.

in which we can escape the danger of Allied air attack,' he continued, 'and that is to attack by night, resting during the day or getting in so close to the enemy that his airmen dare not risk attacking in case they hit their own people.' He turned to von Dodenburg. 'That is where you come in, my dear Colonel.'

General Hausser smiled at the young commander of SS Assault Regiment Wotan, pleased with what he saw. Von Dodenburg was the finest type of SS officer, intelligent, loyal, and careful of his men's precious lives, not like so many of his younger officers, who were all brawn and no brain, and who were proud to report higher than normal casualties after each attack. If anyone were capable of carrying out what he had in mind, it would be von Dodenburg and his Wotan.

'How, sir?' von Dodenburg queried.

'Like this. You are to be given the honour of leading the attack. Here,' he tapped the map, 'at Mortain. It is defended by a battalion of the U.S. 30th Infantry Division. Not one of the Amis' best divisions, according to Intelligence, and its members are pretty exhausted after the last two weeks' fighting.' He shrugged slightly. 'The Amis obviously have no idea of how long the average German soldier has to spend in the line, but no matter. Now, von Dodenburg you will lead the attack on Mortain at one o'clock on the morning of 7th August. With luck, you should be in the town itself by first light. Once you are in the place and closely engaged with the enemy, their high command will be unable to use their Jabos. In that sort of confused fighting, they wouldn't dare take the risk. Now, once darkness falls on the night of the 7th, the 1st and 2nd SS Panzer Divisions will push in 120 tanks along a ridge of high ground – here – between the valleys of the Rivers See and Selune. Both of the rivers will provide natural flank cover against enemy ground interference. My commanders of the SS will, I am sure, be capable of covering the distance between Mortain and Avranches by daylight on the following day.'

Both Lammerding and Wisch of the 1st SS barked in

unison, '*Jawohl!*', as if it were the most obvious thing in the world.

'In essence, then, von Dodenburg, what I am asking from you and your Regiment is to take Mortain by dawn on the 7th, and hold it till nightfall. Just one last Tiger or Panther in Mortain by darkness of the 7th and Wotan will have completed its task.' Hausser paused, his single eye glowing with both pride and tenderness as he gazed at the handsome, blond Colonel who epitomized all that was best in the Armed SS. 'And remember, my dear von Dodenburg, if we lose this battle, we lose France, and if we lose France . . .' He shrugged and did not complete the rest of the sentence.

But von Dodenburg did not need him to do so; he knew what the lean, one-eyed general meant. *If Germany lost France, she would undoubtedly lose the war* . . .

TWO

'I don't like it. I don't like it one bit,' General Leland Hobbs, Commander of the 30th U.S. Infantry Division, complained as he crouched in the forward observation post of his 120th Infantry Regiment's positions. 'For all the Sam Hill we know, half the goddam Kraut army could be lying in wait out there!'

The Commander of the 120th Infantry, crouched next to the over-weight general, said nothing, while the young major who commanded the 2nd Battalion continued joylessly to whistle the current hit, *Straighten up and Fly Right*, through his front teeth.

Once again Hobbs swung his glasses from left to right, trying to penetrate the darkening *bocage* countryside, while behind him the sun slipped further and further beyond the horizon. And again he could detect nothing. The fields, hedged in by the tremendously powerful thickets which had proved such a trial to his weary infantry these last two

20

weeks, were silent and empty. Indeed, the only sign that there was still a war on was the silent flickering of the faraway artillery barrage.

Hobbs frowned. For the last fourteen days his doughboys had been battering their bloody way through the *bocage*. Yesterday Bradley had assigned him this sector of the front, giving him the task of holding the Avranches hinge, with the fate of Patton's whole Third Army depending on his weary, understrength division's ability to hold the dozen or so miles which separated their positions from the sea. Yet he was completely in the dark. Sibert, Bradley's Intelligence Commander, had been able to tell him virtually nothing about the enemy to his front. Indeed there had been something strangely reticent about the handsome ex-West Point Professor when he had asked him for information, as if he had been holding something – something very frightening – back.

Hobbs lowered his glasses and rose ponderously to his feet. The two subordinate commanders followed his example, glad that within minutes the bad-tempered general would be on his way back to his own HQ. 'Don't like it, Major,' he barked to the young Battalion Commander. 'I've said it once, and I'll say it again, I don't like it one bit.'

'Sir,' the young Major replied routinely.

'Keep those doughs of yours on their toes tonight. Use stringent measures. I don't want anybody goofing off to the village to try to raise himself a piece of frog tail. And threaten to have any sentry who goes to sleep on duty put up against the nearest wall and shot. 'Kay?'

'Sir.'

Hobbs stuffed his binoculars into their leather case. 'I'll dine with you tonight, Sutherland,' he said to the colonel. 'What's on the menu at your CP?'

'S and S, sir,' Sutherland replied, stifling an inward curse at the thought he would have to suffer the divisional commander's company for another hour or two.

'*S and S!*' Hobbs moaned, while behind his back the young battalion commander grinned; he knew how Hobbs loved his belly. 'Shit and shingle *again*[1]. Can't your goddam hash slingers think of anything else than that?' With a sigh he slid out of the forward observation post, followed by the others, leaving the darkening French countryside silent and somehow sinister behind him.

'Well, I'll piss up my sleeve – an Ami general!' Matz whispered, as they watched the three Americans crawl back along the hedge to the place where they had hidden their jeep. 'I bet he'd be worth a seventy-two hour pass in Pig Alley, Paris and a piece of French slit, to the Führer.'

'And you'll be worth a good slam around the spoons in a minute, if you don't cut off the air, you poisonous garden dwarf,' Schulze snarled, sprawled next to him in the tall, already wet, grass. 'Knock it off. Do you want the whole goddam Ami army to hear you?'

'Get off my eggs, Schulze, or I'll make the lice in yer pubic hair dance the can-can.'

'You and whose army, corkscrew-cock?'

'Shut up, both of you rogues,' von Dodenburg, lying between his two veteran and most trusted NCOs, hissed urgently. 'Save your energy for the enemy.'

'Those ink-pissers of Amis, Colonel?' Schulze sneered contemptuously. 'All they can do is write propaganda pamphlets asking us to surrender. You'd think they were trying to fight us to death with crap-house paper.'

Von Dodenburg flashed Schulze a hard look. The words dried at the NCO's thick cracked lips.

Carefully von Dodenburg raised his night glasses, shading the lenses with his free hand, just in case, and focussed them on the infantry positions just behind the Amis' forward observation post.

The Americans had established themselves in a loosely linked series of one-man foxholes on the far bank of a shallow-looking little stream. There was no depth to the line, as if the Amis were very thin on the ground and were being forced to stretch their manpower. All the same, their com-

[1] The GI name for hash on toast.

22

mander had dug in a 57 mm. anti-tank gun, covered by little machine-guns, on each flank. The two anti-tank guns were no problem, von Dodenburg told himself. Their armour-piercing shells would bounce off the steel glacis plate of his Panthers like ping-pong balls. Still, he knew, the m.g's could cause problems. His Panzer Grenadiers would have to ford the stream in front of the tanks, giving the armoured monsters cover from the American bazooka-men, who could be deadly at close quarters at night, and the m.g's would wreak havoc in their ranks. They would have to be knocked out first if he were going to limit casualties and achieve surprise. After all, as Hausser had said, the whole operation depended upon speed and surprise. He daren't use artillery to knock the m.g's out in advance. Other means would have to be found.

He lowered his glasses, and rolling round on his back, looked up at the blackened faces of his two NCOs. 'See those m.g. nests at ten and sixteen hundred hours?' he asked.

Matz and Schulze nodded in unison, very businesslike now.

'It would be very useful if they could be knocked out before the attack starts – *quietly*. Any suggestions?'

In a flash Matz whipped out his deadly little knife, an unholy smile on his black wizened face, while Schulze, more slowly, pulled on a pair of enormous brass knuckles.

'My little crippled friend with his pig-sticker and me with my Hamburger Equalizer should be able to do the job, sir,' Schulze grunted. 'Indeed, you can consider it done. I'll take ten o'clock. Parrot-prick here can take sixteen hundred.'

'*Alone?*' the colonel asked incredulously.

'You don't think we'd risk our necks with that pack of warm brothers and knobbly-kneed boy scouts masquerading as soldiers backing us up, sir, do you?' Matz said, jerking his head in the general direction of Wotan's positions. 'I'd sooner risk my arse in a male Turkish bath than take that kind of a chance.'

23

Von Dodenburg laughed softly. 'All right, the two of you, have it your own way.' He dug out the two Very-light pistols from his belt. 'Take these. Green means that you have succeeded in carrying out your mission.'

'When exactly, sir?' Schulze queried, slipping his knuckle-duster back in his pocket again.

'Midnight. We'll kick off the attack then.' He looked down at his issue wristwatch. 'You'd better—'

'Circumcize our watches,' Schulze beat him to it; he knew the routine formula by heart.

Again von Dodenburg laughed, and then, businesslike, the three of them agreed on a time.

Von Dodenburg took one last glance at the enemy positions. They were outlined a stark menacing black against the blood-red half-orange of the setting sun. Carefully he rose to his feet and looked down at the two veteran NCOs. 'All right, you two, I'm off now. And listen,' there was genuine affection and concern in his voice, 'take care of yourselves, do you hear? I want to see your stupid mugs at dawn tomorrow.'

'Easy as falling off a log, sir,' Matz said.

'You can't kill weeds, sir,' Schulze said. 'You'll have Mrs Schulze's handsome son on your back for a long time to come.'

'Let it be that way then. *Hals und Beinbruch!*'[1] The next instant the young, black-jacketed Colonel had disappeared into the growing gloom.

THREE

'I gets to this town, see, and just friendly-like offers one of them frog gals a piece o' gum. I didn't think nuthin' of it. But she busts out cryin'. So I give her the whole goddam pack . . .'

Stealthily Schulze parted the thick clump of bullrushes

[1] Literally 'break your neck and bones'. Roughly, 'happy landings'.

at the water's edge, grateful for the noise of the stream, which covered any sound he made, and viewed the scene as best he could in the poor light.

The crew of the anti-tank gun and their comrades from the m.g. were sprawled asleep in their foxholes.

'Like a bunch of crap-arsed kids in their cradles,' Schulze told himself. 'Easy meat for Mrs Schulze's son and heir.'

There were only two sentries, one with a carbine over his shoulder, leaning against the slim barrel of the 57mm. doing the talking, the other listening, while he spooned out hash from the can he held, with the lazy motions of a man who knew he had long hours of guard duty to kill and was in no hurry.

Schulze nodded his approval of the set-up. The two of them would be first. Then he would tackle the sleeping beauties. He began to crawl forward again.

'Then I sez, does she want to have some chow and a drink? And she sez, sure, but it's gonna cost me plenty on the black market. So I sez, Christ on a crutch, what's the good of dough if you don't spend it . . .?'

Schulze was about five metres away from the two of them. Carefully he pulled on his Hamburger Equalizer. Then as an afterthought he loosened the stick grenade which was stuffed down the side of his left dice-beaker. He might need it quick in an emergency. He crawled on.

'So we had a swell meal, steak and the rest of it and plenty of dago red and cognac. It all came out to about ten bucks. But it was worth it, because when I get her outside the restaurant, she can't wait to get back to her room for a jig-jig and we done it up against the nearest wall, right off the main drag, you know, butterfly fashion and then – and it just goes to show what pigs those frog dames are – she bent down and . . .' The sentry stared at his companion, who had suddenly frozen, spoon poised at his lips, his eyes wide and round. 'Hey, don't you want to hear what that dame did to me next?' he demanded, a little angrily.

'The . . . there's . . .' the other man's attempt to speak

ended in a strange strangled sound, as if he were being slowly garrotted to death.

'What the Sam Hill?' the man with the carbine swung round, following the direction of the other GI's petrified gaze. 'Oh, my sweet ass . . .' They were the last words he ever spoke.

The gigantic stranger in the camouflaged tunic of the SS, with the frightening silver SS runes glittering at its collar, launched himself out of the darkness. Schulze's brass knuckles connected the sentry's upturned jaw. There was a harsh click. The sentry's head shot back. Blood spurted in a thick jet from his smashed mouth and nostrils. He fell as if pole-axed, his neck broken.

Beyond him the other man awaited his fate tamely, too frightened to move, the only sign that he was still alive the oddly twitching mouth, already dripping with the saliva of fear.

Schulze's big ham of a fist lashed out. Metal struck metal. The GI's spoon buried itself deep in his gullet. The GI sank to his knees choking. Schulze had no mercy. He caught the GI's helmeted head, steadied it, and jammed his knee into the American's chin. In his agony, the GI bit the spoon in half. He sank to the ground without another sound.

Schulze gasped for breath. Two down, four to go, he told himself. But there was no time to be wasted. The man nearest him was stirring uneasily in his sleep. Humming Brahms' *Cradle Song* to himself, Schulze raised his right dice-beaker and brought it down with all his strength on the man's upturned face. One hundred and eighty pounds of brawn and muscle drove the regulation thirteen hob-nails of the dice-beaker's sole deep into the sleeping man's face. 'Sleep, baby, sleep,' Schulze sang through gritted teeth, as the man's spine arched with pain before he fell back unconscious into a suddenly blood-filled pit. Schulze rushed to the next man, who was just beginning to open his eyes, alarmed by the noise. Schulze launched a tremendous kick at his face. The bone structure smashed like a too-thin eggshell tapped by a too-heavy spoon. The GI went back to sleep again – permanently.

In rapid succession, Schulze dealt with his two remaining 'sleeping beauties.' But now there were sounds of alarm coming from the rest of the line of dug-in Amis. Schulze slipped the stick grenade from his boot and pulled out the china pin which armed it.

Dark shapes were beginning to run towards him. He waited till they were in range, then with all his strength he hurled the grenade at them. The potato-masher swung through the darkness in crazy circles and dropped right in the middle of the leaders. There was a thick muffled crump. Violet flame split the night. Mangled bodies, bits of limbs, flew in all directions and the sudden rush came to a halt. Schulze hesitated no longer. Raising the Very pistol, he pulled the trigger. There was a soft wet plop. The flare sailed lazily into the night air. *Crack*. Suddenly the startled GIs saw outlined in that sickly green light, the gigantic figure of a lone SS man laughing at them uproariously, as if they were some tremendous, crazy joke. But not for long. Just as the flare started to sink to the ground like some fallen angel and the hell of war descended upon them, the SS man flung himself down behind the nearest ·30-calibre m.g. Next moment, angry white tracer started to zip through the velvet darkness. The battle for Mortain had commenced!

Three hundred metres away, Matz observed the green signal flare just as he had completed slitting the last Ami's throat. Carefully he pulled off the leather gauntlet with which he had protected his right hand from injury during the lethal operation and looked down at the pale blur of his fingers, as if he were seeing them for the very first time. 'What a bunch of pretty little chaps you are,' he said affectionately, 'and how you've sprung up since I last saw you.'

The sound of running feet and the sudden angry, alarmed cries alerted him to his danger. He forgot his hand. Grasping the pistol, he, too, fired the green 'success' flare, before dropping behind the BAR automatic rifle and directing a well-aimed burst at the men pelting towards the crewless anti-tank gun.

'All right, Gent, you know what to do,' von Dodenburg said rapidly, as the twin green lights rose on the horizon.

Captain von der Tanne, commander of the Panzer Grenadier company, known behind his back as 'Gent' to his admiring young troopers, jammed the cracked monocle he affected into his right eye and raised his swagger cane, his only weapon, in a kind of salute. But the look of sudden pain on his thin face belied his jaunty air, and von Dodenburg knew why: the white gloves he always wore hid two pink claws, all that remained of his hands, burnt off by a flame-thrower during an attack on Kharkov by the *Bodyguard* in 1942.[1]

'I know, Colonel. My chaps and I will take a little stroll over that ditch yonder, crack a few heads of the gentlemen from across the Big Pond and then hurry on to catch up with the – hopefully – waiting tanks.'

'Correct,' von Dodenburg snapped.

His plan envisaged the two heavy tank companies – commanded by 'Yid', Captain Abraham Rosenburg, nicknamed thus on account of his highly suspected Hebrew features and his pathological hatred of the Jews; and 'The Professor', Captain Heinrich Hellmann, who had been a pre-war elementary schoolteacher and had been trying to live down the disgrace ever since – turning the flanks of the American positions under the cover of a direct attack by von der Tanne's troopers, backed up by the company of Panthers, which he, von Dodenburg, would command personally.

'Remember, Gent, that the essence of the whole attack is to get through the Ami line quick and seize the exit road leading westwards to Mortain. There will be no time for

[1] SS Panzer Division *Adolf Hitler's Bodyguard*, to which Wotan had originally belonged.

mopping up. Leave that to the stubble-hoppers of the *Wehrmacht*, who will follow us.'

'Naturally, my dear Colonel,' Gent answered with affected haughtiness. 'You don't think I'd let my chaps soil their hands on too many Amis? They might even catch something.'

Von Dodenburg's face wrinkled into a brief smile and he laughed. Gent was remarkably cool, although he knew that he and his young eager grenadiers would be wading the thigh-deep water of the stream in a few moments under direct *Ami* fire. All the same, he was living up to his motto that 'a gentleman is always a gentleman, even with his trousers down – and he must know how to die gracefully.'

'All right, on your way,' von Dodenburg said, and kicked his own driver in the small of the back to start up. 'And the best of luck.'

Von der Tanne touched his swagger stick to the peak of his cap and yelled, *'Bugler!'*

'Sir!' The bugler snapped smartly above the sudden roar that the Panther's huge Maybach engine made as it came to life, flooding the night air with the nauseating stink of diesel oil.

Gent said, 'Sound the charge, bugler, please!'

Von Dodenburg shook his head; von der Tanne certainly did things in style. Then as the young captain raised his swagger cane and cried, 'Follow me girls, the captain's got a hole in his arse!', he dismissed Gent and his charging grenadiers from his mind and concentrated on his own task. Touching his throat mike, he called, 'Report One.'

Metallically distorted, the voice of the commander in the furthest Panther answered: *'Fertig, Obersturmbannführer!'*

'Report Two!'

Swiftly each tank commander reported that his vehicle was ready for action. Then, as the river line erupted in a wild crackle of small-arms fire, von Dodenburg pulled down his goggles, took a last look behind him, and yelled over the intercom, *'Wotan – vorwaerts!'* With a great roar of 400 hp engines, the metal monsters, weighed down by their

29

huge, overhanging 75mm. cannon started to waddle forward into battle.

FOUR

'Great flying buckets of shit!' Schulze exclaimed, as a burst of machine-gun fire zipped frighteningly just above his head and the first of Gent's Panzer Grenadiers tumbled into the slit trench next to him, panting hard. 'What the hell took you wet-tails all this time? If I'd have known you were going to make all that fuss about crossing that streak of piss, I'd have dealt with the Amis on my lonesome.'

'We took pretty bad casualties,' the boy gasped, his face streaked with blood. 'Half the noncoms were hit . . .'

'No bogging down there, laddie,' von der Tanne's high-pitched voice cut into the young trooper's explanation. 'We can't have any of that sort of thing. Into the breech, you know . . . And you, Sergeant-Major Schulze, surprised to see a veteran like you skulking in a nasty hole. Ought to set a better example to the chaps, what?' Gent swung his swagger stick in the direction of the Americans, who were falling back more rapidly, now that they knew their flanks had been turned by the speeding German tanks. 'After them, laddies. Remember every American has a lovely sweet red arse-hole. *Charge!*'

Enraged by von der Tanne's comment, Schulze grabbed the ·30-calibre machine-gun, and cradling it in his big arms, stumbled forward after the officer, firing from the hip as he went.

'Shittingwell skulking in a shitting hole,' he grunted. 'I'll show the sodding fairy bastard!' Angrily he fired a rapid burst, narrowly missing von der Tanne and felling half a dozen GIs to his immediate front, who hit the ground in a mess of flailing arms and legs.

Now von Dodenburg's Panthers were beginning to ford the body-littered stream, its waters already running blood-red, their engines making a murderous noise in bottom gear. Von Dodenburg's tank waddled up the muddy bank and, just in the nick of time, missed Corporal Matz, who was busily engaged in prising gold teeth out of the open mouth of a dead Ami infantry lieutenant.

'Great God and all his triangles,' the little man protested angrily, as the Panther's whirling tracks showered him with pebbles and mud. 'Can't a bloke indulge himself in his hobbies? I don't know – there's no peace for the wicked.' He pulled the 'flatman' from his hip pocket, drank deeply, belched with pleasure, and then applied himself to the difficult task of trying to prise a lump of gold from the dead man's right wisdom tooth.

Von Dodenburg swung his eyes from right to left on constant lookout for a lurking Ami bazooka-man who could spell disaster for the Panther in this hand-to-hand type of combat at night. To his right, a completely naked GI was hanging from an apple tree, while at its foot, among the mess of ripe apples disturbed by the impact of a tank shell, another dead GI lay sprawled extravagantly, with what looked like a piece of 75mm. shell sticking out of his naked arse. But von Dodenburg had no time for the bizarre casualty. Two khaki-clad figures were running crouched through the apple trees, and one of them carried a three-foot long tube. He slapped his throat-mike. 'Bazooka-men, fourteen hundred hours!'

The young gunner needed no urging. He swung the turret round in a flash. The co-axial machine gun chattered. White and red tracer stitched a trail of death through the gloom. The leading man flung up his arms, his hands flapping wildly. He hit the deck. Next to him the GI with the bazooka raised his deadly weapon and tried to balance it across his shoulder. The gunner, sweating with fear and apprehension, didn't give him a chance. The co-axial burst into frenetic action once more. The GI went down, his body almost sawn in half. The Panther rolled on over the lifeless bodies.

A shell ploughed into the orchard directly to von der

Tanne's front. Apple trees came tumbling down like broken matchsticks, pelting the helmets of the advancing grenadiers with apples. *'Deckung – volldeckung!'*[1] Gent roared.

'Balls to that for a lark!' a still-enraged Schulze cried. While the young troopers, their eyes wide with fear, their hearts hammering frantically, buried their faces in the debris-laden dust, he sprang forward. Ignoring the shells which were beginning to rain down on them now, filling the air with red-hot, hissing shards of gleaming deadly metal, he pelted towards the abandoned Ami anti-aircraft Bofors. With one leap he was in the aimer's seat, crazily twirling the twin handles to bring the barrel down. In a flash he had the muzzle horizontal. He pulled the firing lever. The anti-aircraft gun, now working in a ground role, roared into violent life. A great wall of red and white fire reared up in front of the pinned-down troopers, as the hail of 37mm. shells sped towards the Ami artillery positions. It cut down all before it, turning the orchard into a flaming, all-consuming monster, driving the artillery men from their positions, making them scuttle, panic-stricken, for safety before the flames consumed them, too.

'On your toes, my lucky lads,' Gent yelled, waving his cane, knowing that his grenadiers must take advantage of the respite immediately, before fresh Ami artillery zeroed in on them. 'Let's see those legs open wide. Don't worry – nothing will drop out. I'll vouch for that.' In the lead once more, he sped by a sweating Schulze, crying, 'Not bad, Sergeant-Major. But don't let's bog down now, what?'

'Oh, you aristocratic arse with ears,' Schulze cursed to himself. 'What do you want me to do to prove myself? Cut off my sodding arms and club the sodding Amis to death with 'em?' He dropped out of the gun-layer's seat and charged after the Panzer Grenadiers disappearing into the fiery smokey gloom.

'Hit the tube, driver!' von Dodenburg snarled over the intercom. The young driver pushed his foot down hard on

[1] 'Take cover'.

32

the accelerator. The Panther burst forward through the orchard, squashing and pulping the dead and dying bodies of the defeated Amis which lay everywhere. Maybach engines screaming at full power, the blood-red tracks whipped up great clods of mud and earth. Skilfully the driver manoeuvred the forty-ton tank onto the *pavé* road. To its right a burning farmhouse suddenly caved in, showering the advancing Panzer Grenadiers and fleeing Amis with bloodred sparks. In the very last instant, Matz, clutching a bottle of Calvados and a great looted ham to his skinny chest, ran up the Panther's forty-five degree glacis plate, swung over von Dodenburg's head and flopped down gratefully on the rear deck. Von Dodenburg had no time to wonder where the little one-legged corporal had come from and how he managed such a feat with his wooden stump; he was too concerned with making contact with the heavy tank companies on both flanks.

Pressing the throat mike, he repeated time and time again, 'Big Bear One . . . Big Bear Two . . . Do you read me . . .? *Do you read me, for God's sake?*'

Suddenly the metallic distorted crackle of the ether was broken by a harsh bitter voice. 'I read you, Big Bear, I read you, Big Bear.'

It was the Yid.

'Big Bear Two, what is the situation?' von Dodenburg rapped anxiously. 'Report . . . report.'

'Road free . . . road free,' Captain Rosenburg could not conceal his mood of triumph. 'To my front the whole gang of Jewish businessmen and gangsters are running for their precious lives. They're creaming their breeches all along the front. Over.'

'Excellent . . . excellent,' von Dodenburg cried excitedly, overcoming his dislike of Yid, who he suspected had once been a member of Himmler's infamous 'extermination commandos' in Russia before he was transferred to the Wotan. 'Good work, Big Bear Two . . . Halt and prepare to take a little friend on board. Over and out.'

Von Dodenburg pulled off his earphones and grabbed

the signal pistol. Behind him on the swaying deck of the armoured monster, Matz was slicing off large chunks of the looted ham, swallowing them ravenously (although he had not yet wiped the knife, with which he had slit the four Americans' throats) and washing the fatty meat down with greedy gulps of the fiery apple brandy. For all the world, he looked like some contented picture-goer, watching a particularly exciting movie. Von Dodenburg raised the pistol and fired twice. A green flare, followed an instant later by a blood red one. It was the signal he had agreed upon with Gent. It meant Gent was to break off the fight and join the heavy tanks. The line of the U.S. 30th Infantry Division was broken. *The road to Mortain and the sea was open!*

FIVE

A GI came running out of the burning red darkness. He was laughing crazily. Suddenly he was aware of the long column of sinister black Panzers. With a scream he threw away his rifle and dropped to his knees, kissing the cobbled road in front of him. Then he began to scream again. Scream and scream and scream.

Yid flicked on the turret searchlight. The screaming, crazy GI was pinned down in a circle of hard white light. 'Stop that foolishness, you Jewish pig!' the SS Captain commanded harshly. 'Stop that screaming!'

The GI continued to rant, the saliva running down his unshaven chin and dripping onto his blood-stained, ripped shirt, his body rocking from side to side with the effort, the veins sticking out ugly and swollen, purple at his throat.

Yid hesitated no longer. He seized the handles of the turret m.g. Hardly sighting the weapon, he pressed the trigger. At a rate of 800 bullets a minute, the first salvo ripped the GI in half. 'Die, Jewish swine,' Yid cried and kicked the driver in the small of the back. 'Advance, you idiot, *advance*, and run right over the American animal.'

34

There was nt even a slight bump as the Tiger's tracks ground over the dead man, tearing his body to shreds and leaving the helmeted head attached to one of the links, until a bogie knocked it off and it went rolling down the cobbled road like an abandoned football.

The advance to Mortain went on.

The young Panzer Lieutenant saw too late the men lurking in the ditch. Three bazookas roared simultaneously. Purple flame stabbed the blackness. At that range the Americans couldn't miss. All three rockets hit the Tiger with a tremendous metallic boom. White-glowing shards of steel flew high into the air. Within the tank, the crew were killed instantly by the shock wave, while the young lieutenant, minus both his legs, fell to the ground and then began to hobble on the bloody stumps towards the horrified Americans, waving his revolver, his screams rasping on their nerves.

Burning oil spurted from the ruptured Maybach engine. It ran after the dying lieutenant like a red wave, and engulfed him. In an instant, his upper body was a sea of flames. Still he kept on moving, while the fiery tongues of red rose ever higher. It was too much for the bazooka-men. They flung away their weapons and screaming crazily they ran to the rear, right into the fire of the waiting Panzer Grenadiers. *Mortain was only five kilometres away now.*

The Panthers thunderd through some nameless hamlet. The heat from the twin exhausts and the carbon-monoxide fumes had sent Matz and Schulze into a semi-conscious trance. Matz did not even notice the parade of lice across his wizened face, as his body-vermin crept ever closer to the blessed heat; and Schulze clutched a bottle of Calvados in his paw, still virgin and untouched.

Abruptly the dark, shuttered houses blazed with fire. An anti-tank gun thundered. A dark figure scuttled across the *pavé*, dragging a chain of Hawkins grenades behind him. The Panther at point was hit simultaneously by a 57mm.

35

anti-tank shell and the explosion of the Hawkins grenades' daisy-chain.

Immediately the Panther gunners went into the well-remembered routine. While the Panzer Grenadiers vaulted expertly over the steel sides of their halftracks and doubled to the rear of the American-held houses, scuttling up the walls and drainpipes like monkeys to break into them through the roof, the tank gunners systematically blasted the windows and doors of each house.

Within a matter of minutes it was all over. The hamlet was a mass of searing white flames – one of the houses was a distillery – and the frightened survivors were being rushed to the rear by Gent's exuberant young troopers.

Matz opened his eyes. 'Schulze, you know somethin'?'

Dreamily Schulze looked across at his running mate sprawled full length on the swaying metal deck. 'What?' he said thickly.

'Combat makes me horny. I've got a stiff salami.'

'So?' Schulze said, lazily tilting the bottle to his cracked, dry lips.

'I fancy dipping my sausage in a little bit of hot mustard sauce.'

Schulze guzzled the apple brandy sloppily, allowing half of it to dribble down over his massive unshaven chin. He belched and said, 'Everybody in the Regiment knows you don't like girls, Matzi.'

Lazily Matz nodded. 'Yes, I must admit there's one or two nice lookers in the new batch. But I ain't got no vaseline.'

'Use axle grease like you always do,' Schulze suggested, yawning loudly. A moment later he was back in the drugged trance, not even aware of the slugs striking the turret above his head with the noise of heavy tropical rain on a tin roof.

It was still dark, and Mortain was just two more kilometres away.

'Oh blast,' the 'Prof' said in that pedantic prissy schoolteacher manner of his. The screaming clang of the explosion on the side of his Tiger told him all he wanted to know. His company had run into trouble.

Down below, an oil lead burst. It drowned the cabin in stinking heavy oil. Slowly the Tiger rumbled to a stop. The Professor cleaned his pince-nez the best he could and chanced a look over the turret.

Outlined against the scarlet stabs of artillery fire, he could see grey shapes coming crawling out of the woods to his right. American tank destroyers armed with great 90mm. cannon which even outgunned his own 88mm.! He ducked down again and pressed his throat mike. 'Gunner, enemy SP's at fourteen hundred. Now, don't panic. Remember what I've always taught you. Cool, calm and don't jerk the firing bar.'

The gunner busy wiping the thick stinking oil off his sweating young face told himself that the Professor could stick his advice up his dried-up schoolteacher's arse, and whirled the turret round frantically. Behind them the long line of stalled Tigers did the same. The gunners who managed to get the first round away would win this encounter, they all knew that.

'Fire at will,' the Professor commanded.

'Fire up your arse!' the gunner said to himself, and jerked back the firing bar.

The 88mm. erupted into violent, ear-splitting life. The AP[1] shell, white-glowing and ghostlike in the gloom, hissed through the night, cutting a burning path through a clump of trees and striking the leading tank destroyer directly in the side. The countryside reverberated with the great metallic boom. The tank destroyer swayed from side to side like a ship caught by a sudden typhoon. For a moment nothing much happened. Then the M45 flew apart in a metal cloud, great gleaming shards of bent and buckled steel hissing hundred of metres through the night air.

It was almost as if a signal had been given, a call to battle. The whole line of the stalled Tigers opened fire. The broadside swamped the slower tank destroyers. Flames engulfed

[1] Armour-piercing.

them. Infantry which had taken cover behind them fled, their uniforms already burning, some of them running in panic-stricken, screaming circles. The sweating Tiger gunners in their glowing metal boxes changed to high explosive; the SPs were finished now. Shell after shell rained down on the infantry. An anti-tank gun disappeared in one thunderous detonation. When the smoke cleared again, what remained of it swung from a birch tree in an oddly lazy manner. Mushrooms of black oily smoke were ascending to the pre-dawn sky everywhere now. The American infantry, those still alive, were falling back with ever increasing speed.

The Professor clamped his throat mike tightly with well-manicured fingers. 'I'm going to transfer to Number Two now. I want you men to remain with the vehicle. Please ensure that you do your utmost to get it running again. You know how badly we will need as many runners as possible this day. Now remember what I have just said, men,' he ended prissily.

At his seat, the gunner gave a loud, long, juicy, contemptuous fart. The Professor adjusted his gold-rimmed pince-nez more firmly – he wore it in imitation of his idol, *Reichsführer* SS Heinrich Himmler, who had also been trained as a teacher – and dropped over the side. On the horizon, dimly outlined by the first dirty white of the false dawn, he could see the tall Gothic spire of Mortain's church. *They were nearly there now.*

'Off the road, driver!' von Dodenburg commanded.

The teenager down below in the tank's interior did not hesitate. He had complete confidence in his young commander. The Panther careered off the *Pavé*, lurched into the ditch and then, with its engines roaring ear-splittingly, it thundered up the rise into the wet fields beyond.

Von Dodenburg manned the turret m.g. There were Americans everywhere. Most of them were fleeing for their lives back to the little French town, but he couldn't chance some desperate Ami having a crack at the Panther column with a bazooka. One wrecked tank would block the whole road. Soon it would be dawn, and dawn, he knew, would bring the *Jabos*. He could not afford to be trapped out in the open in daylight. Swinging the machine-gun from left to right, he fired short, accurate bursts at the men in olive-drab uniforms, speeding them on their crazy flight through the fields, not giving them a chance to turn and fight.

Below in the turret, the gunner had understood why they had rolled off the road so suddenly. He started firing too, HE mixed with phosphorous shells. Americans fell everywhere, their melodramatic dying gestures clear in the brilliant white light of the burning chemical. The Panther rolled forward over a carpet of twitching bodies, mashing and kneading them into the blood-red mud.

A GI, braver than the rest, let the huge metal monster roll over him, then grabbed for its rear. By mistake he caught hold of one of the burning hot, fiery-red exhausts. There was an overpowering stink of burning flesh. The GI fell back, screaming piteously, his hand burnt away to the wrist.

Another desperate soldier tried the same trick. Lazily Schulze kicked him in the face. He tumbled beneath the huge flailing tracks. They tore off his legs and flung them high into the air like carelessly thrown garbage.

A frantic group of GIs tried to set up an anti-tank gun. Von Dodenburg's gunner beat them to it. Even before von Dodenburg could swing round the turret m.g., he fired, a yellow-red spurt of evil flame. Black smoke rolled upwards in a fantastic mushroom. The gun flew apart. Bits and pieces of human flesh rolled across the field. A body whacked against the Panther's glacis plate and burst like an over-ripe melon. Blood and gore splashed Matz in the face. Groggily he wiped the red mess from his cheeks, saying, 'Schulze, I think, it's coming on to rain.'

'Ay,' Schulze, still deep in his fume-induced semi-coma, agreed. 'Now St Peter's gonna piss on us as well.'

The Panther came to a track. A 57mm. shell whacked into its steel side and bounced off like a white ping-pong ball. The Panther reeled like a drunkard and fought to remain upright. Desperately the teenage driver struggled to keep the 40-ton vehicle from overturning. Von Dodenburg fired a wild burst in the general direction from which the shell had come. But he knew the gun was not particularly dangerous and there was no further time wasted in trying to knock it out. 'Turn up the track, driver,' he commanded, 'we'll join the road again up there.'

The Panther swung round in a clatter of pebbles and earth. American wounded came hobbling and crawling towards them, throwing away their helmets and raising their arms in a token of surrender. The gunner didn't give them a chance. He fired. A torn-off head of one of the surrendering GIs landed with a wet plop between Matz and Schulze. The big NCO looked dazedly at the bespectacled head, complete with helmet. 'Well, I'll shit in my boot,' he concluded finally. 'That's a funny kind of a hailstone.'

Matz giggled stupidly.

'Stop firing now, gunner,' von Dodenburg commanded swiftly. 'They can't harm us.' He glanced over the side of the turret, as they waded through shattered bodies, staring grimly at the puckered, mangled flesh, with silvery white bones sticking through the blood-red gore and purple-grey snakes of entrails hanging out, and flattened faces with the eyes staring back at him, as if in eternal accusation. He swallowed hard and looked away. *Before him was Mortain*.

The halftracks and tanks of SS Assault Regiment Wotan rattled through the little town. The windows of the houses were shuttered tight, but von Dodenburg got the impression that there were frightened people hiding behind the shutters, peering through the cracks, ears glued to the doors, alert to the slightest danger. Dead Americans lay sprawled everywhere, like carelessly abandoned bundles of rags. A jeep was burning near the town hall. Panzer Grenadiers were breaking down the doors of shops with their rifle butts. Others were looting the dead Amis, shouting with delight, like children at a lucky dip, when they discovered cigarettes or candy. From somewhere there came the sound of a woman screaming, and von Dodenburg frowned. He could guess what that meant: some of the battle-hardened veterans of combat on half a dozen fronts were taking their own personal reward for the hardships of battle. They were beginning to rape the local women.

He pressed the throat mike. 'Stop here, driver,' he commanded.

The Panther, its metal side dripping in blood and gore, rattled to a stop outside the *mairie*, where a frightened pot-bellied Frenchman, with red and white mayoral sash across his bulging stomach, was already pulling down the Stars-and-Stripes and the *Tricoleur*, which were hanging from the second floor window. Lightly, Schmeisser machine-pistol in his hand, von Dodenburg dropped over the side and called up to the still groggy NCOs, 'All right, you two rogues, make dust, we'll set up our HQ . . .'

The rest of his words were drowned in the frenetic scream of many engines. He flung a glance upwards. From the west a myriad of silver-painted single-engined planes were zooming in towards them, their fat bellies laden with bombs. He grinned in spite of the terrifying noise. It was the feared *Jabos*. But they were too late. *Wotan had beaten them to Mortain.*

SIX

Holding the vital signal in his hand, which he had just received from the SLU[1] commander, Winterbotham hurried across the wet grass in the still silent HQ towards Bradley's caravan. It was only barely dawn. But he knew he had no other alternative than to wake the 12th Army Group Commander.

[1] Each major allied commander had a 'Signals Liaison Unit' attached, made up mainly of British personnel, which received the decoded German Enigma messages and passed them on to the commander.

He hesitated, and then knocked at the door of the caravan.

'Come in,' Bradley answered immediately and opened the door himself.

He was already wide awake, washed and freshly shaven, but his red-rimmed eyes showed he had spent a sleepless night. 'Morning, Winterbotham, what about a cup of Joe?' He indicated the big thermos of coffee on his desk.

Winterbotham shook his head. 'In a minute, sir, if I may. But I think I should show you this, first.'

'Ultra?'

'Yes sir and top priority.' Winterbotham tendered the flimsy to Bradley, but the bespectacled Commander shook his head.

'My poor old eyes ache like hell. You read it please, Winterbotham.'

'Very well, sir. It's from Hitler to von Kluge. As you know the attack went in last night—'

'Yeah, I know – to my cost,' Bradley said a little bitterly. 'Hobbs' poor old 30th Infantry took a bad knock this night. The Krauts – that Wotan outfit you mentioned – are in Mortain.'

'Well, sir, that's what the message is really about.' He bent his blond head. 'It reads "I command the attack to be prosecuted daringly and recklessly to the sea, regardless of the risk." Hitler then goes on to say that he has to "remove all remaining Panzer groups from the Falaise front facing Montgomery and to commit them to the Avranches. There they are to attack in order to bring about the collapse of the enemy's Normandy front by a thrust into the deep flank and rear of the enemy facing the German Seventh Army." He ends the thing with a bit of pseudo-Churchillian rhetoric, stating "the greatest daring, determination and imagination must give wings to all echelons of command. Wotan has shown the way, the rest must follow, with every man believing in final victory. The battle cry is 'Wotan leads, we follow.' " ' He sniffed. 'End of signal.'

For a moment there was a heavy silence in the caravan.

From outside there came the sound of jingling dixies and cooks' ladles. The 'hash slingers', as the GIs called them, were beginning to prepare breakfast for the HQ.

Finally Winterbotham broke the silence. 'Well, one thing is clear. Ultra has not been compromised. Hitler is still using the Enigma to relay his messages, and he is still prepared to press home his attack to the hilt, obviously completely unaware that we can read his orders by radio as swiftly as poor old Field Marshal von Kluge himself.'

Bradley's gloomy face brightened. 'So that means I'm in the clear, Winterbotham, eh? I can turn on the heat now?'

'Yes sir. Ultra is safe and I'm completely sure the PM would have no objection to whatever military action you took now. You can lay it on with a trowel, if you want.'

'That's all I want to hear,' Bradley said excitedly, his night-long gloom vanishing instantly. 'All right, Winterbotham, go and grab yourself some chow. I've got some work to do now – *fast*.' He grabbed for the scrambler phone, Winterbotham, the bringer of the good news, forgotten. The last words the tall British Secret Service officer heard as he left the caravan was Bradley's order to the operator, 'Get me General Patton – and get him fast, Corporal!'

'Georgie – Brad. Morning.'

'Morning, General,' Patton's well-known, high-pitched voice came across the air. 'Hell, I didn't know you goldbrickers at HQ got up at this time of the morning like us poor, flat-footed doughs.'

Bradley ignored the usual Patton attempt to take a rise out of him. Once he had been Patton's subordinate; he knew all the tall, grey-haired Third Army Commander's tricks. It was useful knowledge to have, now that he was Patton's superior. 'Listen, Georgie, we've been hit during the night – *bad*.'

'Where?'

'Mortain.'

'Sweet whistling Jesus!' Patton exclaimed, the cheery note vanished from his voice.

'Yeah, and that ain't all. There's more to come – a helluva lot more of it, to the tune of all the armour on Monty's front.'

'Hell, if I'd have been the Field Marshal,' Patton savoured the title of his hated rival, 'I'd have wiped out that Kraut armour long—'

'Shut up, Georgie, and listen,' Bradley interrupted Patton before he went into one of his usual tirades against the Britisher. 'We know from British Intelligence that the other fellow is committed to a full-scale armoured attack towards Avranches. Now, that attack has its dangers, but also its potentialities. If the Kraut breaks through, you'd be cut off, though Eisenhower has already promised me two thousand tons of air supply to you a day if that eventuality ever occurred.'

'Yeah, if the Limeys don't get their hands on them first. You know what I say – Ike[1] is the best general the English have.'

'Knock it off, Georgie, and listen,' Bradley said brutally. 'That's the danger. But there are incalculable, highly attractive potentialities. Von Kluge is sticking his nose into a trap, risking his élite divisions to do so.'

'You mean,' Patton said eagerly, 'that instead of going over to the defensive at Mortain, we let 'em keep on coming, getting ever deeper into the bag, while we continue to advance and swing round behind them to cut them off.'

'Right in one, Georgie. Now our Intelligence can no longer be compromised, I'm putting in two extra divisions at Mortain, so that the Krauts can't advance any further, and as soon as their armour starts moving today to link up with their point at Mortain, I'm going to loose the flyboys on 'em. They'll sic out those Kraut Panzers.'

'Hot dog,' Patton cried exuberantly. 'It'll be slaughter, beautiful massive slaughter!' An instant later, the exuberance vanished from his voice. 'But what about the Field Marshal and his Limeys? Can they move fast enough to grab Falaise so that I can link up with them and trap the

[1] Nickname for General Eisenhower.

Krauts? You know the British, they spend half the time brewing tea and polishing their brasses?'

'Don't worry about Monty, Georgie,' Bradley answered soothingly. 'He's already alerted. His Canadians are starting their attack in the direction of Falaise this morning. They'll form the left part of the jaw once they've captured the place, and your doughs will form the right. And listen, I don't want you advancing further than Argentan. You could easily run into Monty's men coming from Falaise and there'll be hell to pay if Allied troops started firing on each other by mistake.' He paused. 'Remember, Georgie, a commander only gets an opportunity to destroy a whole enemy army like this once a century. It'll be a great victory.'

At the other end Patton sniffed audibly. 'Not with the Field Marshal making the running, Brad,' he said sourly. 'Why don't you let me and my Third Army go for Falaise? We'll drive the Limeys back into the Channel for another Dunkirk and finish off the Krauts at the same goddam time. This stopline at Argentan is no more use to me than a pecker is to the Pope!'

'Georgie, can't you watch your big mouth?' Bradley exclaimed in despair. 'Thank God this is a scrambler line or we'd have to apologize to the Vatican.'

Patton chuckled. 'If you think that's bad, Brad, you should hear some of my remarks about the kikes.' Then he added hastily, 'OK, that's it then – stopline at Argentan. But I'm warning you, Brad, you'll be sorry. Monty will let the Krauts escape.'

Bradley laid the phone down carefully and stared into nothing for a moment, listening to the sounds of the awakening camp – the rattle of the cooks' pots, the stamp of the MPs as they raised Old Glory with military precision, the noise of the message jeeps being warmed up for the usual flood of after-breakfast messages – and thinking over the plan. Everything had been set in motion. There was nothing else he could do. Slowly he rose to his feet and stared at the big map, covered in red and blue pencil marks which indicated the positions of his own and the enemy's units.

THE COUNTER-ATTACK OF SS ASSAULT REGT. WOTAN, MORTAIN, FRANCE, AUGUST 1944.

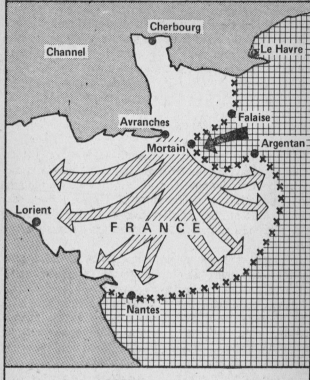

His gaze fell on the furthest red mark, located at Mortain. He screwed up his red-rimmed eyes and made out the name once more. '*SS Assault Regiment Wotan*' he read the designation softly out loud.

For a moment he did nothing. Then on sudden impulse, he reached for the sponge and began to rub the name out. By this time tomorrow, he told himself, *SS Assault Regiment Wotan* would be flying for its life . . .

SEVEN

With elaborate ceremony, Sergeant-Major Schulze took out a magnifying glass and peered down disdainfully at the little piece of hard 'Old Man',[1] which the red-faced, bald-headed Quartermaster Sergeant had just offered him with a slice of black bread. 'And pray what is this, Quartermaster Sergeant?' he asked in what he called his 'Sunday best' accent.

'You know shitting well what it is, Schulze,' the Quartermaster said angrily, 'your shitting breakfast ration and there's cold coffee – nigger sweat to you – to go with it, if you want to know the worst.'

'If I didn't know better,' Schulze said slowly, dropping the lump of sausage onto the cobbles of the square outside the *mairie*, 'I would have sworn that it was the dried-up dropping of a Jew with a very small arsehole.'

'Well, what do you expect?' the Quarter protested. 'My only two supply halftracks got caught on the road in by the Jabos. The morning goulash is now spread from here right back to Vires. You're soddingly well lucky to get the Old Man, believe you me.'

'And?'

'And shitting well what, Schulze?'

The big Sergeant-Major looked down at him. 'Well, don't tell me, Mr Head Kitchen-Bull, that you are thinking of

[1] Hard sausage, reputedly made of dead old men.

47

feeding that kind of crap to my boys today. If you do, you can start moving your well-upholstered quartermaster's arse to the infantry straight away, 'cos that's where you're going to end up before your big paddle-feet can hit the deck.'

'But . . . but . . .' the unhappy NCO protested, 'where can I rustle up any grub in this God-forsaken dump with the artillery coming in every minute as if they got a dose of the trots on the other side of the line and the Jabos banging away at anything and everything that moves?'

'Personally I can feed my guts with German Army dice-beakers and wash them down with goat piss and still feel contented. But not my lads, Quarter. They're funny that way. They want exotic grub like pea soup with lining, or sauerkraut and sausage. Even a bit of bread and a hunk of cheese seems to appeal to their perverted, decadent tastes.' He ducked instinctively as another 155mm. Ami shell hit the outskirts of the little town and sent a huge column of debris sailing into the air. 'Can't hear yersen speak,' he commented routinely, and went on, 'Thus, my fatassed friend, get on the stick and see what you can loot in the way of grub from the Frogs, or,' Schulze's voice sank so that it sounded like a load of gravel going down a metal chute, 'I'll slice off your eggs personally with the bluntest bayonet I can find and make a meat fricassee of them.'

The Quarter fled. Ignoring yet another 155mm. which socked into the western edge of the little town, only a matter of a hundred metres away, Schulze, well pleased with his morning's work, sauntered back across the debris-littered square, to the regimental HQ.

The Gent, Yid and the Professor were all assembled in the CO's Command Post, the Mayor's own shabby office, complete with a notice dealing with drunkenness in youths under 18 and an old portrait of Marshal Petain, to replace that of General de Gaulle, which had decorated the cracked, dirty wall the day before.

Schulze swung a tremendous salute to von Dodenburg sitting behind the burgomaster's desk, and bellowed, 'Sergeant-Major Schulze reporting, sir!'

Von Dodenburg winced. 'Don't you think you can tone your voice down to a dull roar, Schulze? Those Ami 155mm.'s are bad enough as it is.'

'Sir!'

'All right, what's the food situation?'

Schulze allowed himself an unholy grin. 'If the Quartermaster Sergeant knows what's good for him, sir, the boys will be eating fresh French bread and good Norman butter with a dab of strawberry preserve for breakfast in spite of the fact that the supply halftracks bought it. Otherwise, Captain von der Tanne, there will be an immediate volunteer for your Panzer Grenadier company.'

Von Dodenburg and Gent grinned. Yid for his part frowned – he had no sense of humour – and the Professor's face retained its puzzled look; the ex-teacher, von Dodenburg couldn't help thinking, always looked puzzled.

'Good, good, Schulze.' Von Dodenburg waved to them to take a seat. 'All right, gentlemen, let us have a look at the situation.' There was a murmur as the others settled in their chairs. 'Now, in spite of the fact that the Amis are banging away with those damned cannon of theirs from the heights to the west of Mortain – they must have unlimited ammunition – it doesn't appear that they are softening us up for an attack.'

'No stomach for fighting, that Jewish rabble,' Yid commented sourly.

Von Dodenburg ignored the remark. 'Seemingly our attack must have really caught them with their knickers down.'

'Save for the jolly old *Jabos*,' Gent reminded him lightly. 'They certainly gave our kitchen bulls a nasty headache an hour or so ago.'

'You can say that again, sir,' Schulze agreed. 'There'll be no more owl-shit cooked in this town for a while. The suet soldiers can rest over their goulash cannon for a while. Thank God.' He crossed himself with mock reverence.

'So what are we going to do?' asked von Dodenburg. 'My orders were to hold on to Mortain till nightfall, when we

49

will be joined by the 1st and 2nd SS Divisions, to make the drive to Avranches. General Hausser personally ordered me to take no risks. All I had to do was to hold this place. However, we are not the asphalt soldiers of the Bodyguard.[1] We are Wotan, and Wotan does not hang around contemplating its navel when vital objectives might be achieved at low cost.'

'You mean the heights, I presume, sir?' Gent beat von Dodenburg to it before he could spring his little surprise.

'Yes, I do,' the young Commander answered, a little chagrined.

'But, once we leave the outskirts of town, sir,' the Prof protested, 'the *Jabos* will be upon us. I mean, I am prepared to try to cure my throat-ache as much as the next man,' he fingered his neck, undecorated by the medal of the Knight's Cross as were the throats of the other four, 'but I don't think I envisage suicide as a suitable means of obtaining the medal.' He gave the CO one of his rare mouse-like smiles.

'Of course, not, Captain. As long as I have commanded Wotan, I have never ordered men to risk their lives heedlessly. Every action must have a fair chance of success without too many casualties. No, gentlemen, this is what I have in mind. As you know, the reason why the Amis are limiting their bombardment of Mortain strictly to artillery is because their own infantry are dug in close to the western outskirts of town. To use the *Jabos* on us would be too risky. Any dive-bombing attack might well hit their own lines.' He turned to Gent. 'How many Amis did your troopers put in the bag, Captain?'

Gent was caught off guard by the unexpected question. 'A hundred, perhaps one hundred and fifty, sir,' he replied. 'My laddies didn't have time to count them accurately. I'm afraid they were too busy getting their greedy paws on as many cancer sticks as possible.' He slapped the swagger stick against the highly polished riding boots, complete

[1] Known as asphalt soldiers because most of their duties before the war consisted of parading before foreign dignitaries in Berlin.

with silver spurs, which he also affected. 'Why do you ask, sir?'

'Well, I was thinking we should get rid of them. They are useless mouths to feed and besides, if General Hausser's plan works out, we'll soon have a whole army of Amis as POWs.'

'But that, of course, is just a cover for something else,' Yid snapped. 'What do we care whether that khaki rabble starves or not?'

Von Dodenburg shook his head in mock sadness. 'You are a very distrusting individual, Captain Rosenburg. I can see you do not think I am motivated by humanitarian considerations, eh?'

Yid said nothing.

'Well, you are right. You see, if we let the Ami prisoners loose to cross back to their own lines, their artillery and whatever *Jabos* there are about will be forced to stop firing and bombing. Obviously they won't want to hurt their own people.'

'And then?' Yid rapped, sallow face suddenly flushed with suppressed excitement.

'And then,' von Dodenburg answered, while the others leaned forward to catch his every word, 'we do this . . .'

When he had finished outlining his bold plan, there was a moment of silence, broken only by the steady pounding of the Ami 155mm. cannon.

Yid spoke first. Clicking his heels together, as if he were on the parade ground, skinny body rigidly at attention, he barked, 'Permission to volunteer, *Obersturmbannführer*?'

Prof, well aware that the Knight's Cross he might win in such a daring action would stand him in good stead for promotion in the post-war education world – they might even make him a headmaster – barked a fraction of a second later, 'Permission to volunteer for the action, too, *Obersturmbannführer*?'

Lazily Gent waved his cane at von Dodenburg. 'Me, too, I expect, sir,' he said languorously. 'Family tradition and all that. Three hundred years in the Prussian service, what!'

Von Dodenburg looked at their keen young faces and then at Schulze's broad, tough, working-class face, brick-red with good health, the summer sun, and many years of schnapps. Schulze's gaze seemed to be focussed on some object that he could see far beyond, through the smashed window. The Colonel grinned. Schulze was too experienced to play games like Yid and the Prof.

'I'm afraid, gentlemen, I can't take all of you with me. Mortain must be held at all costs and I can't afford to risk your heavy Tigers, Rosenburg and Hellmann. They'll be needed for the drive to Avranches this night. General Hausser will need all the muscle he can get. No, you two will remain behind here. You will take over command, Rosenburg, as senior officer, and hold the town.' He turned to an apparently bored Gent, who was swinging his swagger cane back and forth, as if time hung very heavily on his hands. 'I'll take you with me, von der Tanne.'

'Lor', what a treat,' the young crippled Captain simpered in an affected falsetto.

'And you, too, you big rogue,' von Dodenburg said to Schulze. 'Ass-hole tight – I can't stand the smell of shit!' was Schulze's sole comment.

EIGHT

Now it was mid-day. Under the burningly hot August sun, obscured now and again by the smoke cloud caused by the explosion of another 155mm. shell, the unshaven, sweating Ami prisoners shuffled around in scared confusion, their eyes on the SS guards who had herded them at bayonet-point to this exposed part of the town.

'They're gonna gun us down,' some said fearfully. 'Ner,' others replied more confidently, 'the Kraut bastards are gonna do a trade. Exchange us for some of their own guys that we've got in the cage.'

But most of the prisoners were more concerned about

their raging thirst; many hadn't had a drink since their capture the night before, and they held up dirty cupped hands or empty canteens, crying, 'Water . . . *eau* . . . *wasser*. Hey, you guys, what about a drink?'

But the young tankers stared at them, wooden-faced and motionless. All of them had been well briefed. Everything had to go strictly according to plan. Exact timing was essential.

Yid looked at his overlarge gold watch, which he had taken away from a Jewish banker just before he had shot him in Poland during his service with the SD execution commando, and nodded to the waiting Prof. 'The Colonel will be in position now, Captain. You can talk to the degenerate pack now.'

Hellmann adjusted his pince-nez more firmly, and looking down from the deck of the Tiger, cleared his throat and said, 'Please, everyone, listen to me.'

The jumbled mass of GIs turned, hearing someone speak English to them. 'Give us water,' several of them cried, throwing back their heads and pointing their thumbs at their mouths, as if they were drinking from a bottle.

'In good time, you will get water,' the Prof continued in his fractured English. 'Now, you listen.'

'Okay, you guys,' a young lieutenant, with a blood-stained bandage around his head, ordered. 'Knock it off! Let's hear what the Kraut has got to say.' The chatter died away.

The Prof cleared his throat once more as he had done years before when he had finally managed to silence a difficult class and commence teaching. 'On the well-known German humanitarian grounds, the authorities have decided to give you the release. In short time, you shall return to your lines.'

There was a gasp of disbelief, and someone called, 'Go blow that outa ya barracks bag, chum. They'll slaughter us once we leave this dump . . .'

'Yeah, yeah, he's right,' a half dozen excited, scared voices agreed.

The Yid looked down at the sweating, frightened Americans in disgust. He spat in the dust and dearly wished he could order his gunners to fire into their dark, hook-nosed Jewish faces and silence their animal-like noise for good.

The Prof held up his hands for silence. 'Please . . . please,' he tut-tutted, 'we shall get nowheres, if we are making a sound like that. You will not be hurt. Your leaders will go out under the white flag.' He indicated the broom handles, adorned with sheets, which lay stacked in front of the Tiger. 'Your soldiers shall not shoot at white flags.'

Somebody laughed cynically.

'In addition, our own command has radioed your command and they are aware you are coming.'

A new light of hope began to dawn in the prisoners' tired eyes. The lieutenant with the bandage pursed his lips thoughtfully, as if he were considering all possible angles. Finally he said, 'But why should you release us?'

Von Dodenburg had briefed the Prof on how to reply to that particular question. 'Because food to feed you, we have not. In addition, we do not want our regiment to be accused of placing its prisoners in a dangerous spot when your planes begin attack Mortain this afternoon.'

The explanation did the trick. A fat sweating corporal pushed by the lieutenant and grabbed one of the makeshift flags. 'Brother, let me get out of here – but swift! If TAC Air is coming in, Corporal Joe Ritzi for one is getting out!'

Immediately more and more men pushed forward and grabbed the waiting flags. Yid, high up on the Tiger turret, nodded to the guards and cried, 'All right, let the rabble loose!' The first phase of von Dodenburg's bold plan had succeeded.

'There they go!' Matz sang out from his hiding place in the next street.

'I don't give a cup of Yid piss for their chances,' Schulze commented, as he watched the first hesitant ex-prisoners begin their passage to the Ami lines. 'As thick as the average stubble-hopper is, it'll take 'em half an hour to figure out they're shooting at their own blokes.'

Matz flipped away the rest of his cigarette in a contemptuous red arc. 'They're a lot of bush niggers who piss in their mother's coffee, at best,' he snarled.

'They're squaddies, just like us. Only it happens they're wearing the wrong kind of uniform today. Come on, let's make dust. The CO's waiting.'

Swiftly, machine-pistols clutched in their hands, they moved out of the hiding place towards the barn, where von Dodenburg and Gent were standing smoking nervously and trying to kill that anxious wait that always preceded violent action.

'Well?' von Dodenburg demanded.

'They're moving out, sir,' Schulze replied.

'Excellent.' Von Dodenburg swung round. Cupping his hands around his mouth, he bellowed, 'Start up!'

'Here we go for the next performance,' Gent said, and then roared above the deafening noise, 'Best of luck, sir!'

'Same to you, von der Tanne,' von Dodenburg answered, clambering up onto the turret of the lead Panther with its myriad aerials already trembling with the vibrations. He clipped in the throat mike and cried, 'Roll 'em!'

As the Panther rumbled out from behind its cover, the mortar crew in the last halftrack began to fire their mortars. There was a soft plop. The obscene howl of the mortar shell tore the sky apart. Next instant, the first smoke shell broke in front of the departing prisoners, enveloping them in a thick cloud of white smoke almost instantly.

Panic broke out at once. The POWs scattered madly, their eyes wide with fear, fighting and clawing at each other in their urgency. On the other side of the line, the Ami machine gunners, who had been silenced by the sudden appearance of their own troops in no-man's land, opened up once more. Red and white tracer zipped crazily through the ever-increasing white fog, as more and more smoke shells started to land between the two groups. GIs went pitching to the earth everywhere, while others, already sprawled full length, attempted to grub hasty holes for themselves with their helmets, even their bare hands.

Von Dodenburg took one last look at the slaughter of the Ami POWs and told himself that it would be one more war crime to be attributed to SS Assault Regiment Wotan; then he concentrated on the difficult task ahead.

At fifty kilometres an hour, the column of Panthers and halftracks, pitching and swaying violently on the rough ground, headed for the American lines, the men in the last halftrack firing smoke shells all the time to cover their advance. A couple of infantrymen rose from their foxholes in alarm. A Panzer Grenadier halftrack erupted with fire. The two men stopped as if they had suddenly run into a wall. Another popped up from his hole and tried to lob a grenade into the open turret of von Dodenburg's tank. Schulze hit him with a burst. The grenade dropped to the man's feet. As he crumpled he watched its hissing fuse with awesome intensity. Next moment it exploded. When the cloud of smoke disappeared, all that was left of him were, surprisingly enough, his combat boots. From all sides the American m.g. fire grew in intensity. It tore long splinters of raw bright wood from the trees on both sides. It rattled an unholy tattoo on the metal sides of the wildly swaying vehicles.

The lead Panther lurched into an enemy trench. Von Dodenburg, the veteran, knew the enemy must not be given time to think. The first few moments were always decisive. 'Driver – *right*!' he commanded.

The driver swung the 40-ton tank round, as if he were in a skating rink. Schulze just caught the turret ring in time. The Panther waddled down the length of the trench, twirling round at regular intervals, squashing the screaming soldiers crouched there to bloody pulp.

'Hamburger steak[1] for breakfast tomorrow, Schulze,' Matz yelled, as the Panther swung west again and began heading for the smoke-covered heights once more.

The armoured vehicles blundered into the firs at the bottom of the height, snapping them like matchsticks. 'Bale

[1] A kind of rissole, made of mincemeat.

56

out!' Gent roared, as the column's progress started to slow down.

Expertly, his Panzer Grenadiers, in their green-mottled camouflage overalls, vaulted over the sides of their half-tracks and darted forward to tackle the American infantry dug in among the trees. At such close range, fire weapons were no use. The grenadiers relied on their entrenching tools, the blades ground to a razor-sharp edge. Foxhole to foxhole. *Swish*. The shovel coming down in a silver arc, slicing deep into the soft, khaki-clad flesh, blood spurting up in a velvet jet, the writhing bodies screaming and screaming in the blood-slippy undergrowth. '*Medics . . . medics,*' the dying terrified Americans cried. '*Mother . . . mother, please help me, mother!*' But neither medic nor mother could help them now.

A sinister uncanny slobbering came descending from above the trees. A long grating whistle followed. Abruptly the smoke-filled sky was filled with terrifying noise. '*Mortars . . . they're using mortars . . . Mount up, brothers!*'

The Panzer Grenadiers needed no urging. Running straight up the motors of the slowly advancing halftracks, they sprang across the drivers' ducked heads and dropped down into the safety of the metal boxes on wheels.

Not a moment too soon. Everywhere the Ami 81mm. mortar shells began falling between the trees, killing friend and foe alike. A halftrack took a direct hit. Slumped dead over the wheel behind the shattered windscreen, the driver drove his cargo of dead and dying troopers right off the trail, soaring into nothing, to crash into a disintegrating mass of burning metal far below.

The advance went on.

Just in front of von Dodenburg's Panther the earth opened up like the mouth of a volcano. Stone, earth and trees spewed high in the air in a fiery jet. The driver avoided it with a tremendous jerk of the controls. Matz went flying over the side to land on his feet like a cat, just in time to fire a burst into an Ami running towards them, trailing his entrails behind him like ghastly grey snakes. He fell, entangled in his own panting innards.

They came to a small stone bridge across a ravine. The tanks rumbled to a stop. Was it a trap? Were the Americans ahead waiting for them to start pushing their armour across before blowing it up? Gent rapped out a command. Again the Panzer Grenadiers vaulted over the sides of their half-tracks and doubled forward.

At once the waiting Ami machine guns on the other side of the ravine opened up. The young troopers pressed home their attack. Man after man fell, faces upturned in agony, hands clawing at the rays of sunlight which came through the trees. Their comrades sprinted on, without even a glance at the littered dead, and were hit the next instant themselves.

Now the trees were burning. But the handful of surviving Panzer Grenadiers ignored the flames. Goaded on by the strange fancy that once they were across the bridge they would be safe, that life itself, not death, lay on the other side, they clattered over the rough stone and fell on the Ami machine-gunners, bayonets flashing, sharpened spades slicing into soft white flesh and turning it into a blood-red gore.

The Amis broke. Casting away their weapons in their unreasoning panic, screaming incoherently, they fled up the hill, pursued by m.g. fire from the tanks, while the Panzer Grenadiers, utterly exhausted and trembling in every limb, swayed at the edge of the foxholes they had just taken, as if they were graves into which they might fall at any moment.

The tanks rumbled on. Now von Dodenburg could see the summit and the familiar brown heaps of earth among the green which indicated that the enemy was dug in up there. '*Attack!*' he cried over the intercom. He knew he couldn't afford to lose any more Panzer Grenadiers in an infantry attack. This time it would be up to the tanks, even if the Amis did have anti-tank guns dug in up there. '*Gunner, fire at will! Targets of opportunity!*'

The young gunner needed no urging. He knew the risk the Panther was taking in the narrow confines of the forest. He pumped shell after shell of HE into the summit positions, while on the turret von Dodenburg, Matz and Schulze opened up with their automatic weapons.

A bright-red muzzle flash. A strange white glowing object coming wobbling towards the advancing tanks, gathering speed at every moment. Von Dodenburg's driver jerked the Panther round just in time. Von Dodenburg in the turret could feel the heat as the solid, armour-piercing shot hushed by him. The driver in the second tank was not so quick. The Panther stopped with a jerk as if it had run into an invisible wall. A hurricane of fire whipped towards the burning August sky. Huge fragments of white-hot metal whizzed through forest, cutting down men and trees in a flash. Von Dodenburg ducked just in time as a headless body hurtled just over the turret to slam lifeless, every bone broken, into a nearby tree.

'K-Krist,' Matz whispered in awe, 'what'll they fling at us next?'

As if in answer to his question, a whole jeep hit by a round of 75mm. came flying through the forest, distributing long cartons of Ami cigarettes, which had obviously been stored in its back, as it sailed through the air.

'Ferk me stupid!' Schulze said, open-mouthed, 'Father shitting Christmas has arrived!' Eagerly he reached up his big paws and caught a carton of Camels as it sailed over his head. 'Ami cancer sticks,' he chortled. 'Now I can die happy!'

The Panthers hit the Ami line, cannon and machine-guns chattering. Swiftly and expertly, they swung to left and right, ignoring the 57mm. anti-tank shells that hissed through the air everywhere. Turning inwards when they had reached the flanks of the enemy position, they rattled to the centre, running over any trench from which fire still came. The prospect of being crushed to death was too much for the defenders. Everywhere they sprang from their holes, raising their hands and shouting the one word of German that they all knew.*'Kamerad'*.

'Kamerad . . . don't shoot, buddy, I'm givin' up . . . *Kamerad!'*

'Cease fire . . . *cease fire!'* von Dodenburg ordered hurriedly over the intercom.

One by one the metal monsters came to a halt, cannon still aimed at the enemy who were surrendering everywhere, while Gent's Panzer Grenadiers came hurrying up to disarm their new prisoners.

Von Dodenburg dropped out of the turret. His knees were trembling, sweat was pouring down his face and his shirt was soaked black with perspiration. The fight for the hill position had been costly. There were terrible gaps in the ranks of Gent's Panzer Grenadiers. But they *had* captured the valuable hill position. Now the night attack on Avranches should be a walk-over for Hausser's Panzers.

Feeling as if his knees were made of very soft rubber, von Dodenburg walked through the dispirited prisoners towards Gent's radio halftrack. Gent was smoking a Lucky Strike, holding it with difficulty in his crippled hand. 'Congratulations,' von Dodenburg said. 'Your troopers pulled it off.'

For once Gent's habitual flippancy was absent. 'Yes,' he said tonelessly. 'But they won't be able to do this sort of thing much more often.'

Von Dodenburg nodded his agreement and called up to Gent's waiting radio operator. 'Contact General Hausser's HQ. Report hill position west of Mortain captured and held. Confident now of victory. Von Dodenburg.'

'Sir.'

Von Dodenburg turned to a despondent Gent. 'Buck up, von der Tanne,' he urged, with an attempt at a smile. 'This time tomorrow we'll be on the coast, and your lads'll be able to dip their toes in the briny.'

But Colonel von Dodenburg was sadly mistaken in his forecast; for in twenty-four hours' time, von Dodenburg and what was left of SS Assault Regiment Wotan would be running for their lives . . .

NINE

Exactly at three o'clock, some two hours after von Dodenburg had captured the hill position, he was disturbed in the middle of his meal of captured U.S. baked beans and sausage, washed down with strong U.S. coffee of a kind he had not tasted since the war, by an excited sentry.

'Sir . . . sir,' he gasped as he ran in from his observation post higher up the summit, 'they're moving out!'

'Who's moving out,' von Dodenburg snapped, a little irritated by being disturbed in the middle of the best meal he had eaten since the Invasion had started.

'The Amis, sir. They're moving back from their positions to the west of Mortain.'

Hastily von Dodenburg dropped his mess-tin. Grabbing his helmet, he doubled behind the sentry, followed by Gent, to the observation post.

The man was right. Down below, the Americans were pulling back everywhere, hastily leaving their foxholes and piling into waiting convoys of trucks and jeeps, while further to the rear, the dug-in artillery poured smoke shells into the area between them and Mortain to cover their withdrawal.

Von Dodenburg frowned and picked at a piece of sausage which had wedged itself between his teeth. 'Now what do you make of that, von der Tanne?' he asked. 'What in three devils' names are they abandoning their positions there for?'

Gent shrugged eloquently. 'I really couldn't say, sir. As far as I can remember, the terrain is pretty even between here and the coast. I can't think of any better defensive position than the one they already hold.'

'Neither can I, von der Tanne.'

61

The two officers remained at the OP a little while longer, watching the Amis drive about two kilometres from their old positions to begin digging in again. Then they returned to their abandoned meal, puzzled men.

One hour later they were enlightened about the reason for the enemy's surprise move. The heavy hot afternoon silence was broken by the faint hum of many engines, growing louder by the instant. Startled out of a half-doze, they stared upwards. Above, in the electric blue of the summer sky, a great V of silver-painted planes was heading for Mortain, dragging bright-white con-trails behind them.

'Enemy bombers!' someone cried.

Von Dodenburg swallowed hard. There was a sinister yet inspiring majesty about the scene. 'Some poor bastard's going to get a packet soon,' he told himself. Still lazy, and knowing that he and his men were completely safe in the cover of the forest, he wondered idly who was going to be at the receiving end of the bombs. Suddenly his laziness vanished. The silver V was breaking apart. Their bomb doors had opened. From them fall flares, gold against the deep blue. Slowly they began to descend in ever widening cascades, while the bombers broke to right and left and in a great circle began their return journey to England.

'Pathfinders!' Gent cried.

'Yes, damn pathfinders, marking the target. Now we know why the Amis cleared their positions.'

'Yes,' Gent said grimly, as the first of the long stream of bombers which reached all the way back to the English coast appeared overhead. 'They're going to hit Mortain.'

'God help Wotan now,' von Dodenburg whispered, almost as if he were speaking to himself.

Now the first of the one thousand Flying Fortresses, which Bradley had ordered to strike the point of the German advance, started to sail over the defenceless French provincial town. Bomb doors clicked open and the deadly black eggs began to tumble from its fat silver belly, two tons of them in all, a lethal warning of the two thousand tons of high explosive still to come.

For two solid hours the four-engined bombers flew over Mortain. Artillery positions were wiped out, tanks over-turned and buried in the rubble of falling houses, infantry positions were flattened, trapping scores of men under the debris. By early evening, the entire town resembled the surface of the moon, pitted and scarred with craters every-where. By then all signal communications had been cut and overall command was no longer possible. Several of the young troopers went mad under the strain and rushed around demented until they were shot by their own officers or cut down by the great steel splinters which flew every-where.

Frantically Yid tried to regain control, rushing down the swaying streets between the burning buildings, dodging the fountains of earth and rubble spewed up by the bombs, roaring at the handfuls of shocked men he glimpsed through the clouds of dust, to dig in. To no avail.

Just before he was killed himself, he thought Mortain was going to be granted a respite from the bombing. The last of the Flying Fortresses drew away and there was no sound save the cries of the wounded and dying and the fierce crackling of the burning buildings. But not for long. Abruptly, wing after wing of rocket-firing Spitfires and Typhoons of the R.A.F. came zooming in at four hundred miles an hour, evil purple flames already shooting from their striped wings.

The SS officer dived for cover. Too late. The first Spitfire swept over his head at fifty metres, its engine howling frant-ically, dragging a huge black evil shadow behind it. Its wing man, however, did not miss the man sprawled full length in the burning street. His 20mm. cannon chattered crazily. At that range, the pilot couldn't miss. The little shells tore huge chunks out of Yid's body, sending his flesh flying in all directions, and leaving the flayed carcass twitching vio-lently for a few moments until all life fled.

By seven that hot, burning, murderous evening, the Prof

63

had had enough. Witout asking permission from Hausser's HQ, he ordered the survivors to withdraw. But hardly had the battered handful of men and vehicles left the town on the road that led east than the *Jabos* were upon them. Their leader came in so low that a terrified Prof could see the pilot's pale face quite clearly. But he had no time to study it at any length. Two small bombs tumbled from the Spitfire's striped, clipped wings. With a thick crump they exploded directly in front of the lead halftrack, sending it skidding wildly into the nearest ditch and effectively blocking the road. Frantically the panic-stricken drivers tried to reverse into the town from which they had come. But the *Jabos* were already coming in, cannon and rockets blazing. Prof was blown from his turret by the blast of rockets. For a moment he blacked out. When he came to again, however, he found he could no longer see. Screaming piteously that he was blind, he ran crazily down the road, two purple sockets dripping behind the shattered pince-nez, where once his eyes had been. Fortunately for his future in school-teaching, since there is little use for a blind teacher in the educational system, another rocket blew off his legs and within five minutes he bled to death in the ditch into which he was flung.

Behind him on the road, the troopers started waving white towels and sheets at the planes in token of surrender. But the happy young men in blue, with their enormous moustaches and silk scarves, had been waiting for years for a target like this. They ignored the offer of surrender and the slaughter continued.

'My God, oh my God!', von Dodenburg groaned, as he watched the final slaughter through his binoculars, 'my poor men . . . *my poor men.*'

Down below, the burning houses were swaying like gigantic loose back-drops in a sudden wind storm. Corpses hung in the shattered trees. Down in the square the French fire-engine, which had turned out, still had its motor running – he could see the ancient engine throbbing violently

– but its crew in their brass helmets were all dead, naked, for the baking air had scorched away their uniforms, save for their helmets, belts and boots. Here and there, the wounded, civilian and soldier, hopped bare-foot over the glowing embers, supporting their wounded limbs on crutches, spades, rifles, trying to avoid the buildings which were falling on them from all sides.

Von Dodenburg lowered his binoculars, and thought he would never forget the spectacle of that burning town in its frightening, gorgeous hue of yellow, purple and burning scarlet; and never would he forget those screams and howls, of a kind he had not heard before and never wished to hear again.

'Terrible,' Gent said. 'Terrible! The heavy tank companies have gone hop, that's for sure.'

'Yes,' von Dodenburg agreed mournfully, 'Mortain is completely undefended. As soon as it's dark the Amis will start moving in again.'

'But we've still got your Panthers, sir and what's left of my lads,' Gent said, trying to comfort the tall young colonel with the pale shocked face. 'As soon as it's dark and those damned *Jabos* leave, General Hausser's Panzers will move up, and then we'll show them, sir.'

As von Dodenburg had predicted, as soon as darkness began to fall the Americans began to advance towards the still-burning town. In the ruddy glare cast by Mortain, the silent, watching troopers on the height could see them clearly, as they walked in a slow thoughtful line across the scorched wheatfields and pastures. As if mesmerized, the Wotan men observed the enemy's slow progress, watching how they cleared each stone wall with text-book precision before moving across the next field, slowly swinging out into two horns which finally entered, and disappeared into, the burning wasteland, to find only the dead and dying waiting for them there.

But if von Dodenburg's prediction came true, Gent's forecast that Hausser's Panzers would appear as soon as darkness fell proved wrong. In vain the lookouts posted on the eastern side of the height scanned the road along which they had come. The road was empty, save for the smouldering wrecks of the Prof's Tigers, with dark lumps which were bodies scattered all around them.

Von Dodenburg grew impatient. He ordered the Panzer Grenadiers' radio operator to search the air waves for any sign of the expected advance.

For over an hour, the sweating, anxious operator tried the frequencies normally used by the *Wehrmacht* in combat. But they all remained obstinately silent. 'I don't know, sir,' he confessed to von Dodenburg, removing his earphones and wiping the sweat off his red, wrinkled brow. 'I've never seen anything like it. You'd think the whole German Army had disappeared without trace.'

'Try again, man,' was von Dodenburg's sole comment.

Just after midnight, the operator struck lucky. 'Sir, sir, wake up,' he called to von Dodenburg, who was leaning wearily against the halftrack's side, his eyes closed. 'I've got something.'

'What?'

The radio operator pulled off the earphones and offered them to the Colonel. 'Listen for yourself, sir,' he said.

Von Dodenburg pressed the earphones tightly to his head, the voice was so faint. '*Pull back*,' the weak unknown voice was saying. 'For God's sake pull back . . . the whole op is a failure . . .'

The ghostlike voice faded away into nothing; all the radio operator's hurried efforts could not raise it again.

'Well, sir, what do you think?' Gent asked from his position at the back of the halftrack, where he had been dozing, a looted U.S. blanket flung over his shoulders to protect him from the thin summer drizzle which was now beginning to fall.

'It sounded like the real thing to me.'

'Me too,' Gent agreed. 'Why else no Panzers from Hausser's army? The Amis outguessed us here at Mortain and it's on the cards that those damned *Jabos* hit Hausser's

Panzers just as they were beginning to assemble prior to the drive west. The Amis seemed to know our every move in advance. With the way things are in the Thousand Year Reich,' he said the words as if they were in quotes, 'there could be traitors right up at the top – in the Führer's Headquarters itself.'

Von Dodenburg grunted non-committally. His mind was occupied with something else: that overwhelming question of what to do next? If Hausser's tanks were not coming, what purpose could he serve up on the isolated height? At dawn the Amis would certainly attack, and he would sacrifice what was left of Wotan uselessly. But dare he risk withdrawing without orders? Even the renowned commander of the Wotan might not be safe from Hitler's wrath in such a case. He wouldn't be the first senior commander to be shot at the Führer's command because he had pulled back before asking permission to do so.

He frowned, and gazed at the tired faces of his young men, hollowed out to death's heads in the glare that still came from Mortain. Some of them were mere boys, sixteen- and seventeen-year-olds who had faked their ages so that they could have the honour of serving with Wotan. Most of them still didn't shave, and when Schulze had first seen them, he had exclaimed, 'Holy straw-sack, we'll have to indent at the Quartermasters' for nappies and sugar tits for this lot of wet-tails, Colonel.'

Suddenly one of the boys, a lock of damp blond hair pressed tight to his unsullied brow, stirred uneasily in his sleep and groaned, *'No, mother, no!'*

In these last five years of war, von Dodenburg had heard many men, of all classes and ages, moan out loud in their sleep, expressing their subconscious desires and fears. But at that particular moment of decision the boy's cry, whatever its cause, cut through him like a knife, and he knew he couldn't let a child like that die because he hadn't the guts to make a decision.

'Von der Tanne,' he barked, his old confident self again.

'Sir.'

'We're moving back. Rouse the men.'

Gent hesitated. Von Dodenburg mistook the reason for his hesitation. 'Don't worry, von der Tanne, I'll take full responsibility for the withdrawal myself.'

'It wasn't that at all, sir,' Gent corrected him gently. 'I was just wondering whether I dare say "Thank you" for my lads. You've done the right thing.'

Four hours later, after marching through a torn, slashed, scarred French countryside, where everything stank of death and decay, and where the slaughtered Panthers and Tigers of Hausser's army lay sprawled drunkenly across ditches or smoked in the middle of fields, they ran into the first scared German sentry. What was left of SS Assault Regiment Wotan was back where it had started . . .

THE TRAP

'What would the powers-that-be like Wotan to do this time, pray?'

'Not much, von der Tanne, just commit suicide.'

'Is that all? I thought it was something serious.'

> Conversation: Capt. v. d. Tanne and Col. v. Dodenburg,
> August 14th, 1944.

ONE

'Gentlemen,' General Hausser announced very formally, 'the situation is very serious, very serious indeed.'

There was a murmur of approval from the officers gathered together in the farmhouse HQ. Outside, the 20mm. flak was beginning to chatter again, as a fresh wave of *Jabos* came sweeping into the attack.

Hausser did not seem to notice the tremendous chatter of the four-barrelled anti-aircraft guns. Instead, he said, 'The Avranches offensive is already history, a costly failure. Now my main concern is the future of my Seventh Army.' He pinched the bridge of his beaked nose, as if he were very tired. 'I have already asked Field Marshal von Kluge's permission to withdraw. My request has been turned down on the Führer's express orders. Therefore, gentlemen, we must stand and fight until the powers-that-be make alternative decisions.'

Von Dodenburg looked at Hausser contemptuously. The one-eyed General was a good soldier, but he was like so many German generals who accepted orders leading to the deaths of thousands of young men, without protest. A division, a corps, an army is wiped out and the general, who invariably survives, gets himself a new adjutant, a new staff, a new Mercedes, and a new bunch of cannon-fodder to be sacrificed on the altar of absurd, unworkable orders.

'Now,' Hausser was saying, 'Montgomery's Canadians are making alarming progress against 272nd Grenadier, and the 89th Infantry Divisions on my right flank. Yesterday they hit the infantry positions with some one thousand bombers, followed by an attack of over a thousand armoured vehicles.'

There was a gasp of surprise at such numbers from those present.

'Yes, gentlemen,' Hausser said, 'the enemy seems possessed of inexhaustible technical resources. As a result, some of the front-line units cracked, and the Canadians have now penetrated to a depth of five kilometres.'

From outside came the hearty cheers of some lucky gun-crew, drowned by the whine of the last dive of the *Jabo* they had just shot down. Hausser waited for the crash – which jarred the room, making the plaster fall from the ceiling – before continuing. For every *Jabo* the flak shot down there always seemed to be another ten to replace it.

'Intelligence tells me that Montgomery has his 4th Canadian and 1st Polish Armoured Divisions in reserve, ready to exploit this salient,' Hausser went on. 'As a result, we can expect an all-out drive up the Caen–Falaise road at any moment.'

He tapped the big map at his side. 'That in itself is bad enough, gentlemen, but there is – *perhaps* – worse to come. Here on the Loire our scouts are beginning to send in reports of the first sightings of enemy armour – Patton's Shermans. That crazy American cowboy does not seem to have been worried one bit by our attempts to cut him off at Avranches. He has gone on plunging ever deeper into Brittany . . . Now, the question that worries me is this: will he keep going westwards, with the probable intention of taking Paris, or,' Hausser raised one bony finger dramatically, 'will he swing north?'

'You mean, to link up with any breakthrough the Tommies can make up there?' von Luttwitz queried.

'Right.'

'Then if that's the case, the two hundred thousand rather weary bodies which make up the Seventh Army will be caught in a rather nasty trap,' the gross tank commander said in his usual cynical manner.

'Agreed, von Luttwitz.'

'Then all I can say,' Bayerlein butted in in his quick nervous manner, 'is that we ought to get ourselves beyond the River Dives as quickly as big flat feet can carry us, or I can see us all ending up in tins of Old Man.'

There was a rumble of uneasy laughter from the others, but Hausser's scarred face remained stern and unsmiling. 'As I have already said categorically, there will be *no* retreating. So let us have an end to suggestions of that kind, General.' He let his words sink in. Then he said, 'All you gentlemen will hold your fronts. The men will fight to the last round. Not a centimetre of ground must be yielded. Is that understood?'

'Yessir,' they answered in unison, some enthusiastically, like the commanders of the two SS Panzer divisions, as if they still really believed in the tired old formula; others, like Bayerlein and von Luttwitz, routinely, as if they had heard it many times before and no longer believed in it.

'Good. That is all, gentlemen. You may dismiss to your commands – save you, von Dodenburg.'

There was the usual clicking of heels, the salutes by the *Wehrmacht* generals and the loud harsh '*Heil Hitlers*' of those from the Armed SS, and then they were all gone, leaving Hausser alone with the young, tired colonel.

'Perhaps you think I am now going to reprimand you, von Dodenburg,' Hausser began, 'for withdrawing without orders.'

Von Dodenburg said nothing. Outside, the multiple flak had begun thumping again; obviously the Ami *Jabos* had spotted the departing staff cars.

'You know that such a thing is a capital offence, von Dodenburg. Apart from that, the SS fights to the end – last man, last bullet.'

'Wotan's record stands for itself, sir,' von Dodenburg replied with sudden heat. 'Besides, what is the use of sacrificing good men for no purpose? Aren't we scraping the barrel for man-power as it is?'

'I will pretend I have not heard the last few remarks,' the army commander said icily. 'Utterances like that could have even *you* before the firing squad, Colonel von Dodenburg. Be under no illusions on that score.'

'I am not, sir.'

'Good. As I said at the beginning of a conversation which is taking a highly undesirable and treasonable course, I do not want to reprimand you. Indeed,' Hausser's one eye sparkled with sudden warmth, 'I want to give you and Wotan a chance to redeem yourselves—'

'*Redeem*—' von Dodenburg bit off the rest of the angry outburst just in time.

'Yes, redeem yourselves. The 89th Division which is presently taking the main weight of the British attack is an inexperienced formation. It has spent the last three years in Norway getting fat. I doubt if it can stand long against the full weight of Montgomery's armour unless its backbone is stiffened.'

'By Wotan?'

'Yes.'

'Beg the General's permission to remind him that Wotan presently consists of two hundred Panzer Grenadiers and a company and a half of Panthers,' von Dodenburg said icily.

Hausser seemed not to hear the ice in the young officer's voice. 'What you lack in numbers, my dear Colonel, you make up in quality. You are, after all, the élite of the élite – the Führer's Fire-brigade.'

Von Dodenburg said nothing.

Hausser said, 'Von Dodenburg, keep the 89th in place and hold that front. It is vital. Upon it depends the fate of two hundred thousand German soldiers.' His voice weakened a little, and von Dodenburg could see behind the hard professional shell for a moment: Colonel-General Paul

Hausser, too, was almost at the end of his tether. 'Perhaps soon the Führer will reconsider his decision and allow us to withdraw before it is too late. Perhaps.'

Still von Dodenburg said nothing. How many times in these last years had he heard such appeals to his patriotism and loyalty; and how many good men had died in the ranks of Wotan on the strength of such spurious arguments? *'Dank des Vaterlands gewiss'* [1] he thought to himself cynically.

Hausser stuck out his hand. Automatically von Dodenburg took it.

'Von Dodenburg, don't let me down this time.'

'I won't, sir,' he heard himself saying from far away. 'I won't.'

'Well, Colonel?' Gent asked, leaning against the front of his halftrack, swinging his swagger cane idly and watching the snarl and whirl of the *Jabos* in the summer sky above him with bored interest. 'What would the powers-that-be like Wotan to do this time, pray?'

'Not much, von der Tanne,' he answered, raising his voice above the frantic metallic chatter of the quadruple flak. 'Just commit suicide.'

'Is that all?' Gent said languidly, striking his cane against his still highly-polished riding boots so that his silver spurs jingled. 'I thought it was something serious.'

TWO

The shells burst routinely on both sides of the pitted, battle-littered road. Earth pattered down on their helmets like summer rain. To their right the woods echoed with the nervous high-pitched chatter of German machine-guns, answered by the slower, thoughtful hammering of the enemy guns. To their left a farmhouse was burning. An old crone of a Frenchwoman, in a blue ankle-length dress and white

[1] You are certain of the Fatherland's thanks.

73

bonnet, was dragging a dead body to her cabbage patch to dig his grave there. 'To enrich the earth, sir,' she answered, when asked for her reason for that particular spot by Gent in his immaculate French.

The Wotan column rumbled on, on each vehicle two men continually surveying the bright blue August sky for any sign of the feared *Jabos*.

Von Dodenburg in the lead Panther stared at the desolated countryside. It was like the films of the First War that he remembered from his youth. The landscape was blasted and barren, set with broken trees, their branches hanging to the pitted earth like broken limbs; the earth littered with dead men, lying everywhere like bundles of carelessly abandoned khaki and field-grey rags.

At the most the battlefield couldn't be more than six square kilometres, but every centimetre of it seemed to von Dodenburg to be scarred and slashed. Nowhere was it possible to escape the stench of death and decay; and the flies buzzing in thick blue throngs about the open turrets of the smashed Shermans and Mark IVs indicated that there had been no time to hose out the mangled remains of their dead crews.

'Not a very pretty sight,' Gent commented, reading his CO's mind.

'No indeed, and *they* look even worse.' Von Dodenburg indicated the infantry of the 89th Division, their faces still fat from the good food of Occupied Norway, now drawn and ashen grey, their red-rimmed eyes fixed on the front from which the enemy must soon come again. In their fearful anticipation, they did not even raise their heads to look at the armoured vehicles rumbling by on the elevated road above the ditches in which they were crouched.

'Yes, not quite the flower of German manhood,' Gent said, sniffing contemptuously.

'Shitty lot of Sunday soldiers,' Schulze added his comment. 'There'll be more britches filled than Black Heinriches[1] won when the Tommies come—'

[1] SS name for the Iron Cross, 1st Class.

74

'*Jabos!*' an excited cry from one of the young Panzer Grenadier lookouts interrupted Schulze's words. '*Jabos ten o'clock.*'

'Action stations!' von Dodenburg cried swiftly.

The Panzer Grenadiers knew exactly what to do. With frantic fingers, they drew out the readied Red Cross panels, and draped them over the fronts of their vehicles, while the Panthers swung off the road and crashed straight into the nearest wood, turret gunners already swinging up their machine guns ready to meet the attack, if the new ruse didn't work.

It didn't. The clipped-wing Spitfire came zapping in at tree-top height, machine-guns and cannon blazing. 20mm. slugs struck the cobbles in great blue sparks. Bullets pattered off the metal sides of the halftracks.

'Abandon ship!' Gent cried above the hellish chatter and the mad howl of the plane engines.

Expertly the young troopers sprang over the sides of their vehicles, doubling frantically for the cover of the shattered firs.

Just in time. In the same instant that the Spitfires zoomed high into the metallic blue sky, dragging white trails of smoke behind them, the Typhoons came roaring in. Puffs of white smoke erupted at their wings. The rockets were launched. Like a myriad of red, angry, hornets, they hurtled down towards the abandoned halftracks.

The first one was struck. It rocked madly, then turned over, spilling out fuel across the cobbles. In a flash it was burning fiercely, white tracer ammunition zig-zagging crazily into the unfeeling sky.

Another halftrack was hit. Then another. Now it was the turn of the Spitfires again. This time they came with their small 50-pound bombs. Flaps extended, undercarriages down, pointed noses turned upwards, in order to lower their bombing speed, disdainful of the angry ground fire coming their way, they planted their bombs directly on the last halftrack, sending it flying high into the air to block the road completely when it came crashing down again. Now the handful of drivers who had remained with their vehicles could go neither forward nor back.

A fear-crazed young driver, his face a cracked white blur behind the shattered windscreen of his halftrack, swung the heavy clumsy vehicle off the road, successfully managed to cross the drainage ditch, and rattled into the open fields.

The *Jabos* were on to him like a flash. A dozen of them broke formation and went speeding after the escaping halftrack, machine-guns and cannon chattering. Madly the young driver zig-zagged and changed speed, avoiding the lethal lead time and time again. Then his luck ran out. He hit a deep shell hole. With his rear tracks flailing mud and gravel futilely, he attempted to get out. To no avail!

Von Dodenburg pressed the nails of his right hand deeply and painfully into the palm of the other, willing him to break loose, to get out of the trap. But the *Jabos* gave the trapped boy no chance. The cannon-fire of a dozen planes concentrated on the stricken halftrack, some of the Spitfires coming down as low as fifty metres to take a considered, leisurely shot. Bits of metal flew in every direction. The driver's head sailed high in the air. Still they riddled the lifeless body sprawled over the shattered controls, with their fire.

'My God,' Gent whispered in awe, 'I always thought the Tommies were sportsmen, but this is taking the old fox-hunt a little too far—'

The rest of his awed words were drowned in the great hollow boom as the halftrack's gas tank finally exploded, wreathing the vehicle immediately in bright purple flame.

Five minutes later it was all over, and Gent's halftracks were shattered burning wrecks on the elevated road, while the *Jabos* sailed back to their bases leisurely, obviously to enjoy a well-earned English breakfast of bacon and eggs.

Von Dodenburg dropped from the turret of his Panther and found that for the second time in the last twenty-four hours his knees were trembling; and that his clothes were soaked with the sweat of fear. How long could he and his men stand this sort of thing? he asked himself, as he forced himself to walk straight-backed to the burning column. No wonder that the men of the 89th Infantry looked such wrecks! After three years of peace and pussy in Norway, Normandy must seem like hell itself.

He had just managed to get the wounded driver out of the cab of the third halftrack when he had ample proof of just how shaky the 89th was.

Stubble-hoppers with the red trimmings of the infantry on their muddy, torn uniforms came gasping up the road. Most of them were without their helmets, thrown away in their haste to escape from the front. Some were without weapons. All of them were without reason. Overcome by desperate fear and utter physical exhaustion, they shambled towards the lone SS colonel standing in the middle of destruction, his hand clasped automatically to the pistol on his belt.

They came to a ragged halt opposite him and von Dodenburg could feel the whole force of their misery and never-ending wretchedness at taking part in a battle which seemed so one-sided. This was 1918 all over again, the complete breakdown of the German Army, of which his father, the Old General, spoke in hushed tones, a mixture of anger and shame in his shaky, ancient voice.

Instinctively, von Dodenburg tightened his grip on the butt of his pistol. An NCO with a blood-stained bandage around his head saw the movement and dropped his machine-pistol. 'Go on, shoot, Colonel,' he cried in a choked voice. 'Then, by God, it'll be all over at last!'

Behind him, an older man who had lost his boots sank to his knees, howling like a dog. 'I can't go on any longer,' he sobbed. 'The *Jabos* and the artillery – they're driving me crazy . . . *I can't go on!*'

Von Dodenburg understood their misery. How could they have known what was lying in wait for them, when they left the troop-trains from Norway, their pockets stuffed with cheeses and cigarettes instead of ammunition? This was the real shooting war, not the kind of brass-band-and-parades war of the Occupation base stallions. He withdrew his hand from his pistol and, trying to be as casual as he could be, pulled out a thin cigar and lit it, while they stared at him in fearful anticipation. He exhaled a cloud of satisfied blue smoke.

'Don't you think that it's a bit much to expect one lone officer to cope with the whole of the Tommy army?' he said, in a loud, confident voice. 'I know I'm SS, but there's only one of me and a lot of you.' His voice grew warmer, more intimate. 'I know, men, it's hell the first time. But we've all to go through our baptism of fire. I know, back in '39, I creamed my britches right and proper.' He attempted a laugh, and bending down, picked up the NCO's m.p. and handed it back to him. 'Now, Sergeant, what about taking these men in hand and moving them back to their original positions?'

In a daze the man accepted the weapon, and looked down at it as if he were seeing it for the first time.

'Go on, that's a good chap,' von Dodenburg urged in a soft, reassuring voice.

Face still set dazedly, the NCO turned to the others and said, 'Well, you heard what the officer said. Let's get moving.' Reluctantly but definitely, the fugitives turned and trailed back the way they had come, bound for certain death.

Von Dodenburg tossed away the cigar and breathed out a sigh of relief, just as Schulze burst out of the undergrowth, crying, 'What a shower of shit, sir! God help Wotan with that kind of slack-tail holding the line.' He caught sight of von Dodenburg's abandoned cigar, still smoking in the littered roadway. 'Hey, sir, don't say you're letting that kind of white-assed pisspot get you down? I mean to say, you don't throw away lung torpedoes like that, even if the whole sodding German army seems about to put their feet under their armpits and run like hell.'

Von Dodenburg grinned. Nothing, but *nothing*, seemed to get his veterans down. 'Round up the rest, you big rogue, and let's get on to the front, while there's still one left . . .'

The General commanding the 89th Infantry was finished, von Dodenburg could see that. His face was a leaden-grey and the hand in which he held his cigarette trembled violently. The young SS colonel felt sorry for the elderly *Wehrmacht* General. All his military life he had been preparing for this day, and now the worst had happened – parts of his division had simply run away. At the best his career was over; at the worst, he would be courtmartialled and sentenced to the feared military prison at Torgau. Wanting to help the old man, von Dodenburg tried his best to be positive. In a brisk, businesslike manner, he asked, 'Well, sir, where's the house on fire?'

'Everywhere . . . everywhere, Colonel.'

Von Dodenburg attempted a bright smile. 'It often looks like that on the first day, sir. But you know what they say – a soup is never eaten as hot as it is cooked. Now where can I help?'

The General staggered over to his map, covered with a rash of pencil marks indicating the enemy's local breakthroughs. 'Take your pick. They're everywhere.'

Von Dodenburg went closer to the big map. The enemy had made pinprick breakthroughs all along the 89th's front, but there were too many of them to be taken too seriously. It was obvious that the Tommies were feeling the Germans out and it was obvious, too, that their many localized attacks were aimed at trying to outflank the Caen–Falaise road so that they could push in their armour.

Von Dodenburg stabbed his finger at the map. 'How do you stand at Cintheaux, sir?'

The General shrugged helplessly. 'I've got a company of infantry and a couple of anti-tank guns there. But the men won't be able to hold out long. As you can see yourself, the position is already virtually outflanked.'

'All the same, the position does dominate the Caen–Falaise road, sir.'

'Agreed, but what good is that if it is outflanked?' the

General objected wearily, as if all this talk was completely useless now.

'Even if it were outflanked,' von Dodenburg answered thoughtfully, 'covering the road as it does, it would be like a finger stuck down the Tommy's throat. He wouldn't dare advance any further, if Cintheaux were held by a group of able and determined men. Think of Cassino.'

'My men are not the Parachute Division,' the General said. 'They're the fat, frightened products of too much good living in Norway.'

Von Dodenburg clicked his heels together, knowing that he must bring the discussion to an end; the General was a broken man. He would get nothing more out of him. 'Beg permission to take over at the village, sir?'

'As you like, Colonel . . . as you like,' the General waved a careless hand at the SS officer. He slumped down wearily on the ammunition chest which served him as a seat. He didn't look up when von Dodenburg went out.

One hour later Wotan arrived in the little cross-roads village and set about making preparations for its all-round defence against the attack which must soon come.

But not all the members of SS Assault Regiment Wotan were involved with the defence of Cintheaux, as darkness began to fall and the increasing rumble of the enemy heavy guns indicated that they were beginning to soften up the village preparatory to attacking. Sergeant-Major Schulze and Corporal Matz, sitting in the cellar of the schoolhouse which had been set up as von Dodenburg's CP, had other things on their mind, namely Subject Number One, as the men of Wotan were wont to call sex.

'Do you fancy a trip on the banana express?' Schulze asked casually, stuffing a large piece of over-ripe Normandy cheese down his throat and washing it down with a swig of similarly looted red wine.

'With who, for instance? Perhaps that fat-arsed lieutenant of the 89th, who's bound to cream his britches this night?' Matz said cynically.

'No, I mean real female women.'

Matz paused in the act of rolling himself a cigarette with a page torn from a looted Bible. 'What, in this dump? And besides, have you seen your mug? Buy yersen a mirror and take a gander at it. You'd never turn on the light again.' He laughed uproariously at his own humour, pointing an outstretched finger at Schulze's blackened face.

The big Sergeant-Major shrugged casually. 'Oh, well, if you're not interested, Corporal Matz.'

The 'Corporal Matz' did it. The little man looked across at him with sudden interest. 'Come off it, Schulzi. What you got up yer sleeve?'

'Only two Frog slits – that's all.' Schulze looked down at his begrimed fingernails with mock modesty.

'Now don't keep me in suspense, you big ape. I'd like to dip my wick one more time before I go hop.'

Schulze looked conspiratorially to left and right in the empty cellar, as if they might be overheard. 'Across the road,' he whispered, 'in the cellars of those stubble-hoppers' chaindog HQ, they've got two Frog slits who were sniping at those Norwegian heroes yesterday. They're gonna fit 'em up for a nice wooden box tomorrow morning at six.'

'What a waste, what a very sad waste of womanhood,' Matz said, with a sad look on his wizened face.

'Agreed, my dear Matz. I think the cháindogs should allow them a last request – a sort of hangman's meal.'

'Made up of *your* salami and eggs, I presume, Sergeant-Major Schulze?'

'Correct. I might even allow you to have a jump, though how you could do any normal woman any good with that worm of yours is beyond me. Though I do notice you have very thick lips.'

Matz ignored the insult. 'The idea is excellent, but tell me, birdbrain, how are we to get past the chaindogs? Then why should the frog slits open their pearly gates to accommodate a pair of awful allemans, eh?'

Schulze waited for the roar of an exploding 155mm. shell

to die away before he answered. 'Schulze has got a plan,' he announced.

'Oh, I thought from the look on your fat face you'd suddenly got yer monthlies.'

Schulze sniffed, but continued, 'Now look at it like this, Matzi. What does yer average chaindog want out of his miserable policeman's existence?'

'Promotion, pussy and a fat pension, so he can turn up his flat feet in bed and kick off.'

'Exactly. Thus what happens if a particular corporal of the Military Police receives an urgent summons to report to General Hausser's HQ toot sweet, eh?'

Matz's eyes twinkled. 'He thinks he's got himself a nice safe ball to bowl. Generals never go for a hop in wartime, and there's always promotion on the cards for those base-echelon stallions.'

'That is what I thought, too.' Schulze dug in his pocket and brought out a posting order! 'For one Corporal Kardin, signed by Colonel-General Paul Hausser personally.'

Matz looked at him incredulously. 'Great crap on the Christmas Tree, Schulze, you could get shot for that!'

'It would be worth it for a chance to dip my tail in a little bit of that hot French juice. I ain't had it so long, I hardly know where to look for it any more.'

'Talking about frogs. Once we've got rid of the chaindog and are running the nick oursens, how we going to get them to like us?'

'In your case, I know it's almost hopeless, I must agree on that,' Schulze said slowly. 'With me, my charm, the way I'm built below the belt – in all modesty I have something that used to have the girls on the *Reeperbahn*[1] gasping with eager anticipation—'

'Yes, money.'

'Anyway, to put it briefly, we're going into that cell where they are as two anti-fascist, decent German soldiers who have been sentenced to death for giving their weapons to the brave chaps – the arseholes – of the French Resistance.'

[1] Hamburg redlight district.

'We have?'

'We have, and we're gonna make their hearts bleed on account of our nobility.'

'They'll be ripping their knickers to let us get at it,' Matz chortled in eager anticipation, his wicked little dark eyes sparkling.

'Speak no more, my crippled little friend,' Schulze said, swallowing the last of the Camembert. 'We've got a long night ahead of us. *Vive la France!*'

'*Vive la ferking France* indeed,' Matz echoed, and in high good spirits, the two of them stumped out to carry out their plan . . .

The chaindog, a fat, frightened corporal with the kind of Hitler moustache that marked him as a peacetime SA man[1] was waiting for them impatiently in the shelter of the doorway as they doubled across the battle-littered village street. 'Thought you were never coming,' he snapped in irritation. 'They're probably waiting for me at headquarters, you know, and generals don't like to be kept waiting.'

'Of course, of course,' Schulze said very seriously. 'Sorry, but we had to brief ourselves on the treatment of civilian prisoners, female.'

The corporal slung his pack over his shoulder. 'There's a bucket in the corner if they want to piss and I've already given 'em a hunk of bread and Old Man — that's all you need to know,' he growled. 'Now I'm off.'

'Hope you have a nice time at HQ,' Matz simpered, and watched with distaste as the chaindog edged his way fearfully along the wall to his VW jeep, as if the artillery of the whole British Army was out to get him personally.

'Come on,' Schulze urged. 'Let's get at that lovely grub.'

They hurried inside the abandoned building. Swiftly they unbuckled their pistol belts and dropped them on the table, lit by a solitary flickering candle. Then both of them ripped open their collars and ruffled their hair as if they had just

[1] Stormtrooper.

been roughed-up in the usual fashion of prisoners in the hands of the chaindogs, loudly cursing in German while they did so, before opening the cell door and staggering inside.

The two women were huddled in the straw in the corner of the shaking room, which had probably been a farm labourer's kitchen. They looked up in surprise. One had a huge bosom, thrust out in front of her like a big bass drummer humping up his drum in a military band, and a heavy, hanging chin that would have looked well on a gorilla. The other was petite, brunette and pretty. Both looked very frightened.

Schulze beamed at them. '*Bon soir*,' he said airily, sitting down on the dirty stone floor in front of them and bringing out a pack of cigarettes. '*Fumez*?'

The little one reached out her hand greedily, as if to take the proffered cigarette, but the ugly one, who, Matz could see now, had a definite suspicion of a beard on her Cromagnon chin, knocked her hand away angrily. '*Non,*' she said firmly in a deep bass. '*Sales Boches!*'

'Nix Boche,' Schulze said easily. '*Nous* anti-fascist. *Vive de Gaulle. Vive Churchill. Vive Roosevelt.*'

'You German soldiers?' the ugly one said in broken German, her face still suspicious.

'Yes, German, but hate system.'

'No like system?' the ugly one said, filling her lungs so that her impressive bosom seemed about to K.O. her under her hairy chin.

Swiftly, while the barrage grew in fury outside so that the cell's solitary candle flickered and blew, and threatened to go out several times, Schulze told his story, watching the women's faces for any sign of disbelief. 'So,' he concluded. 'Morning, we put against wall, and firing squad.' He made his meaning quite clear, by squinting through his right eye and clicking his thumb and forefinger as if he were firing a rifle.

His explanation was followed by a flood of voluble French between the two partisans which he could not understand.

Matz took this opportunity to speak for the first time. 'Which is mine?' he whispered out of the side of his mouth.

'Can't yer guess?'

'Not the one with the lungs?' Matz said, horror-struck.

'Naturally, corkscrew-cock. You can borrow a ladder when yer get that far,' Schulze said easily, reaching in his big pocket for the Calvados he had providently brought along. 'Now m'selles, what about a drink to forget it all? Tomorrow we die. Tonight we celebrate. *Bon Santé!*' He took a tremendous slug of the fiery apple brandy and handed the bottle with a flourish to the little brunette, whose eyes were already beginning to sparkle in anticipation.

One hour later, the bottle was empty and the partisans were receptive, both of them cuddled in the arms of their would-be lovers in separate corners of the darkened room. Matz was finding it a little difficult with the ugly one. Reaching up as far as he could, he gave her cheek a peck, to which she reacted with a long, fat groan and *'Je t'aime, mon homme!'*

Even at the peak of his desire, Matz felt like a bluebottle trying to ascend a wall, as he began to climb on top of her and in between her wide-open fat legs.

Across the room, Schulze said, 'Race you, Matz!' and threw himself on top of the pretty one in ecstasy.

But there was no race to be run that night. Just as Matz's skinny frame descended upon the ugly one's large body, there was a tremendous roar. The wall blew in suddenly, showering the two couples with masonry and rubble. Outside, the whole sky to the west was burning brightly.

'*Alarm . . . alarm!*' Gent was crying at the top of his voice. '*At the double!* He blew his whistle shrilling. Suddenly there were running men everywhere.

Schulze dropped off the pretty one reluctantly. 'All right, little one,' he groaned, patting her neat naked bottom, 'on your way. The allemans have to go and get their turnips shot off again.'

The all-out British drive to Falaise had begun.

As the great blood-red ball slid menacingly over the shell-shattered, spiked horizon, the firing stopped. At last that tremendous all-night barrage ceased, leaving behind it a long, echoing silence.

Everywhere the Panther gunners and the grenadiers, crouching in the smoking rubble of what had once been Cintheaux, tensed expectantly. Soon they must come.

Von Dodenburg focussed his glasses. The debris of war loomed up in the twin circles of the binoculars: shattered trees, dead horses with swollen bellies, smoking tanks, and the awkward lumps of dead men. He adjusted them so that he could see further, and caught his breath in a shocked gasp.

'What is it, Colonel?' Gent asked, as he crouched next to him.

Wordlessly the colonel handed the glasses to the crippled captain.

'Oh, my God,' Gent exclaimed, 'I've never seen so many tanks before!' To his startled gaze, it seemed that the whole horizon was a moving mass of steel; there were Shermans and Churchills as far as the eye could see. Rapidly he began to count them, but gave up in despair after he had reached six hundred.

'What –?' he began. But the red flare which hissed into the morning sky made him stop. It hung there a very long time against the pale blue, before finally it descended like a fallen angel to the ravaged countryside. It was the signal the tank armada had been waiting for. There was a sound like a great piece of canvas being ripped apart. Red lights tripped and rippled the length of the horizon. Abruptly the dawn sky was full of the ear-splitting, terrifying tornado of flying steel, and the tanks started to move forward.

Von Dodenburg fought to overcome his fear. 'Von der Tanne, you know what to do?'

Yes, make a neat corpse, the Captain said to himself, but

to his CO, he said, 'Hold the village. You'll take care of the flanks with the Panthers.'

'Yes. Your grenadiers and the 89th's anti-tank guns should be able to stop anything getting through this mass of rubble. My Panthers will—'

He left the rest of his sentence unspoken, but Gent knew what he meant. Twenty Panthers against six hundred enemy vehicles; von Dodenburg didn't have a hope in hell. But there was no use worrying about that now. The battle had begun. Without another word, the two officers doubled to their respective posts. They would not see each other again.

Schulze, commanding the left wing of the Panthers, all ten of them, directed his tank into a hull-down position behind a thick, shattered Norman barn and ordered the driver to nose the Panther deep into the grey stone before pressing the intercom and reporting, 'Hello, Bee One. Wasp One and drones in position.'

Faintly von Dodenburg's voice came over the air, filled with static and the interference of many hundreds of tank commanders reporting in English and Polish. 'Good, Wasp One. Bee One and hive in position, too. Watch those drones of yours keep working. Over.'

'And see you don't get stung, Bee One,' Schulze replied, with an attempt at his usual humour. 'Over and out!'

Now Schulze forgot his CO. A squadron of low-built Churchill tanks, their pennants bearing the bold white eagle of Poland, were lumbering right across his front on the ridge line, clearly exposed and obviously unaware that ten Panthers were dug in in the ruined farmbuildings two hundred metres away. He pressed the throat mike. 'Wasp One to all. Prepare to fire. Pick yer own targets . . . Matz, you ready?'

'What do you think I'm doing? Playing with my marbles? 'Course I'm ready.'

'Right. Churchill ten o'clock. Looks like the squadron commander to me on account of the aerials. Let's tickle up his fat Polack ass with a nice bit o' Krupp steel.'

'Pleasure,' Matz breathed, his eye already glued to the rubber range-finder socket, his shoulder leant against the long 75mm. cannon. The Churchill leapt up suddenly into the centre of the gleaming calibrated glass of the sight. He took a deep breath. The Mark V shuddered. The hollow boom of metal against metal. The Churchill reared up on its sprockets like a bucking bronco at a Western rodeo. It came to a sudden halt, shedding huge chunks of metal everywhere. Next instant its ten-ton turret sailed high into the sky and the air was full of the impact as it hit the ground again.

Matz's first shot was the signal the rest had been waiting for. In a flash, solid AP[1] shot was hissing through the air everywhere. All along the ridge, Churchills were burning abruptly, twisting and turning desperately to escape from the ambush. Two panicked Polish drivers crashed into each other. Others abandoned their still unhurt vehicles to be scythed down by the alert turret machine-gunners. Within minutes, the Polish drive along the ridge had been stopped and the air was full of the stench of cordite, scorched metal – and frying human flesh.

But already the next wave of tanks was battering its way through the burning, abandoned wrecks, as if their crews could not wait to die. 'Holy straw sack,' Schulze cried over the intercom, 'the Polacks must be breeding Churchills like shitting rabbits!' But there was no time to ponder that anatomical puzzle. Already another squadron was coming over the ridge directly at the Panthers, firing as they came.

Still the advancing Shermans had not spotted his Panthers, deeply camouflaged with netting and tree branches at the edge of the wood. Von Dodenburg knew he had an excellent position with a deep depression behind the wood into which his tanks could disappear if the action got too hot. Still, there were so many of them. As far as he could see there seemed nothing but the high Shermans, followed

[1] Armour piercing.

by hesitant infantry. Even at the Battle of Kursk he couldn't remember seeing so many enemy tanks.[1]

He flashed a glance inside the gloomy, green-glowing turret. The red light showed a black FA sign. It meant the 75mm. was cleared for action. He touched the young curly-haired gunner on his thin shoulder to reassure him. 'Don't worry, lad, we'll cope.'

'I'm not worried about us, sir,' the boy replied cheekily. 'It's *them* I'm worried about.'

Von Dodenburg laughed. 'Good for you.'

Then his face grew grim. This was the moment of truth. He could still escape unseen. Once he opened up, however, the whole weight of the Canadian armour would come pressing down on his handful of Panthers. But although the young colonel knew the war was long lost, the old habit of obedience, the iron discipline of Wotan, with its loyalties to the Regiment and nobody and nothing else, made him act as he always acted in such situations. 'All right, gentlemen,' he called through his intercom, 'I think it is time we exercised our calling. *Fire at will!*'

The eager young gunners needed no urging. Like a broadside from an old-fashioned man-o'-war, ten 75mm's spoke as one. There was a sound like some gigantic smith striking a mighty anvil. The first wave of Shermans reeled as if struck by a sudden hurricane. Tank after tank was hit, burning almost immediately, as their highly sensitive petrol engines were struck.

In an instant the crackling radios were full of orders and counterorders in German and English. '*Sherman backing away . . . two hundred, fire! . . . Taking fire from Panther . . . five o'clock. Oh, my God, I'm blinded, I can't see . . . For crying out loud . . . Up a hundred, I said, you four-eyed son-uvabitch . . . Crap in my boot, there's another bunch of the Tommy bastards coming in at eight hundred hours . . . shit, we're on fire.*'

Fire, Fire, Fire. That one terrible word was repeated over and over again in English and German, as the battlefield

[1] See *Claws of Steel* for further details.

89

disappeared in a rolling cloud of yellow acrid smoke. Now the Panthers were beginning to take hits, the poorer quality Sherman shells zooming off their hulls as ricochets, yet frightening the young SS crews so much, as they traced white-hot fingers inside the turrets before they disappeared into nothingness, that they were forced to stop time and time again to urinate into empty shell cases.

Slowly the sheer weight of numbers began to tell. Von Dodenburg caught glimpses of Shermans racing round at top speed, trying to flank him, while the scores of tanks massing to his front tried to pin him down. He knew he mustn't let that happen. The Panthers were very vulnerable from the rear. 'Here Bee One,' he cried over the intercom, while the Canadians tried to jam his frequency, 'to all. Move back . . . Move back position B – *at once!*'

The sweating drivers rammed home reverse. With their gunners still firing at the advancing enemy, they backed down the slope. But not all of them were successful. A Sherman nipping in from the side between two withdrawing Panthers, slapped an anti-tank shell right into the side of one of the Mark V's. The huge tank heeled to one side. Abruptly a great gleaming steel scar appeared the whole length of its right side. A thin white stream of smoke started to streak from its engine cowling. Its gun dropped like a broken limb. Suddenly it exploded with a roar that seemed as if it would never end.

Immediately the fire of nine Panthers was concentrated on the bold Canadian. The Sherman disappeared in a huge cloud of flying yellow and purple, as if it had never existed.

Another Sherman struck lucky. One of its shells hit the track of the last Panther. The broken track flapped behind the 40-ton tank and it rumbled to a sudden stop. Everywhere the Shermans' cannon began to turn in the direction of the crippled German tank. The crew did not wait to see what would happen to them. They flung open the turret and began to bale out.

'The emergency escape hatch, you idiots!' von Dodenburg yelled as he watched through his periscope. 'The escape hatch!'

But the young tankers were too scared to follow the usual drill. They dropped from the turret and started pelting across the littered field. They didn't get far, however. The Canadians were not to be cheated of their prey. Just as von Dodenburg successfully managed to withdraw his command into the cover of the depression, a Canadian Besa m.g. ripped into the fleeing men, bowling them over like nine-pins.

'Two down, eight to go,' von Dodenburg said to himself miserably, as the *Jabos* zipped in over the smoking battlefield in search of the obstinate enemy holding up the great drive. How long could the remaining eight tanks survive?

The whole front quaked and trembled. From end to end the angry blood-red lights blinked like enormous blast furnaces. With a crash the whole weight of the 4th Canadian and 1st Polish Armoured Divisions smashed into Cintheaux. In an instant the hamlet disappeared into the choking grey-yellow fog of burning acrid smoke and flying steel as a thousand shells smacked home.

Gent's grenadiers and the anti-tankers of the 89th Infantry huddled at the bottom of their holes in the ruins, hands clasped over their helmeted heads, bodies drawn up in the foetal position, as the earth swayed and heaved like a ship on a stormy sea.

Everywhere there were hits. Foxhole after foxhole collapsed. Terrified, bleeding, screaming men fought the soil, scratching at the smoking earth with desperate, hysterical claws before they were choked to death. The CP of the 89th gunners was hit. The shattered peasant cottage became a mess of dead and dying men, drowning in their own blood. The captain in charge sat in the smoking ruins, staring curiously at his own legs which, for some reason which he could not comprehend were five metres away from him. Behind him his sergeant lay dying, the old brass crucifix which had been on the wall a moment before skewered through his ample stomach. He died five minutes later, his blood wetting the metal blood of the Man who had died on the cross two thousand years before.

And then, as suddenly as it had started, the tremendous barrage ended. But for what seemed a long time the men crouched in the bottom of the foxholes did not seem aware that the firing had stopped. It was only when they started to hear the cries and moans of the wounded once more that they were aware that the situation was changing.

Gent clawed the earth from his blackened face and slapped his ears a couple of times to stop the terrible ringing. Hastily he sought his cane in the muck and found it. Next moment he jumped out of his foxhole and saw that the world around had been transformed. The village was now a desert of smoking stone waste. But his horrified gaze had no time for the fate of the French hamlet.

Looming up out of the gloom came rank after rank of tanks, followed by slow lines of infantry, plodding thoughtfully across the fields, heads bent as if they were searching for mushrooms. But there were none of the particular mushrooms to stop them that they were searching for – mines. The fields were clear. All that Gent had to defend Cintheaux with were his handful of Panzer Grenadiers and the fat-bellies of the 89th.

He blew a shrill blast on his whistle, 'All right, lads,' he yelled above the roar of the oncoming armada, 'forget the wounded. Back to the firing line. You gunners,' he shouted at the dazed 89th men who were grouped groggily around their 47mm. cannon, 'let 'em come within three hundred metres and then pick off anything with more than one aerial. Those are the command ta—' His words were drowned by the sudden acceleration of the leading rank of Shermans.

'Here they come!' a crazed Panzer Grenadier cried, and opened up with his MG42.

A ragged volley followed from the German line. The Shermans accelerated, showering the plodding infantry-men behind them with mud and gravel. With courage born of despair, the crews of the three remaining anti-tank guns opened fire. Sherman after Sherman came to an abrupt halt and began to burn. Still they came on. The first anti-tank gun was knocked out, its dead crew draped over its bent trails like broken puppets. Still the other two kept on firing.

Now the infantry were running. Gent could see their white strained faces quite clearly and the way their little battle-packs flopped up and down absurdly on their backs. 'Here they come,' he called, and with that courage that had been born of three hundred years of service in the *Offiziers-korps* of the Prussian kings, he stretched himself upright on the edge of his foxhole and waved his cane at the running Canadians. 'Make every bullet count,' he quipped. 'The Quartermaster is being very careful this month.'

And then the Canadians were upon them. A skinny soldier with the jet-black eyes and hair and the pale expressionless face of a Red Indian charged at Gent with his bayonet. Gent stepped to one side and brought his swagger cane down hard on the man's knuckles. He made no sound, but he dropped the rifle all the same. Gent thwacked the cane across the man's face. Still he made no sound. But there was a great purple weal now on the Indian's waxen face. He dived forward and grabbed for Gent's neck. Gent side-stepped and kneed the man. The Indian's face now contorted with pain, but still he made no sound, as he sank to his knees. Gent grabbed his cane in both claws, ripped it round the kneeling man's neck and pulled hard. In the few moments it took him to strangle the Indian, he made not one sound. With his eyes bulging out of his head, his face purple, his tongue hanging out like a pink rag, he went to his death in absolute silence.

Now the Canadian infantry were everywhere among the grenadiers, swaying back and forth in crazy panic-stricken confusion at the edges of the foxholes, hacking and slicing with spade, knife and bayonet.

Gent ripped his spur across the face of a dying Canadian on the ground who was trying to throw a grenade. The man screamed terribly and fell back dead. Gent sprang over him. Ignoring the life-or-death struggle going on all around him, he seized the abandoned Spandau in the nearest foxhole. Standing, not taking aim, unaware of the weight of the m.g., he turned it on the next wave of Canadians. At that range he couldn't miss. The Canadians ran straight into a wall of lead. They were bowled over like a row of toy soldiers struck by the fist of some irate child. Man after man went down.

Suddenly they could stand it no more. The infantry broke, and went flying back the way it had come through and beyond the burning Shermans, fighting their comrades frantically to get out of range of that terrible fire. Gent fired until he could see them no more. Then he dropped the m.g., suddenly aware that his whole uniform stank of burning where the barrel had rested, and turned to the Panzer Grenadiers.

But they had now dealt with the survivors of the first wave and were busily engaged in slitting the throats of the wounded or those who had refused to give up, here and there slamming the brass-bound butts of their rifles into the still figures of Canadians just to make sure that they were really dead.

Gent had to blow his whistle three times before the lust to kill was finally stopped. 'All right, all right, my bloodthirsty monsters, leave something for the crows, will you?' he called. 'Let's get this mess tidied up before they come again . . .'

'*Fire!*' von Dodenburg yelled urgently.

The Panther's 75mm. erupted with a thick muffled crump. The tank shuddered, as the breech block came racing back to eject the smoking brass shell case. Automatically von Dodenburg pressed the smoke-ejector button to clear the turret. To their front, a Canadian Sherman shuddered to a halt. Down below, the gunner tensed over his gun. Should he fire another shell? Nothing happened. No crew baled out, no answering fire, no suddenly burning Sherman.

'Either they've gone hop or they're shamming,' von Dodenburg answered the young gunner's unspoken question. 'But don't waste any more ammo on them. Here come the rest!'

Abruptly six more Shermans loomed up out of the fog of war, obviously confused about the whereabouts of the enemy.

Not for long. Von Dodenburg's gunner worked frantically. The remaining Panthers were obscured by smoke. As far as he knew he would have to tackle the enemy alone. Sweat pouring down his back, his shirt black with it, he pumped shell after shell into the surprised Canadians. Von Dodenburg flung a glance at the shell bins. They were emptying fast. The floor was already littered with shell cases. But he knew they did not dare let up. Once the tanks outflanked them, Cintheaux was finished.

The young gunner struck lucky time and time again. Their front was littered now with burning wrecked Shermans, their crews sprawled burning in the blackened grass or hanging lifeless from the turrets. But now other tanks were bursting through the black clouds of oily smoke to take up the fight, and from beyond von Dodenburg could hear the characteristic crack of a 75mm. which indicated that his other Panthers were heavily engaged too.

Von Dodenburg pressed his throat mike. '*Bee One to all . . . Bee One to all . . . hold ground and keep tight formation . . . keep tight—*' The turret rocked violently. A Sherman had sneaked in from the flank and fired while it was still intact. The round slammed home into the turret, but didn't penetrate. For a moment a startled von Dodenburg watched as the inside of the metal glowed a brilliant white, knowing fearfully that if the round penetrated, they would be dead in a flash. Then the glow had vanished and he was yelling, sweat dripping off his brow like water, 'Enemy tank at nine o' clock – *fire!*'

A moment later the Sherman went up in flames.

But the crew had no time to rejoice about the fresh kill. 'Sherman at fourteen hundred!' the driver yelled urgently. Von Dondenburg spun the periscope round hurriedly.

Another Sherman had sneaked in and was hurtling towards them at fifty kilometres an hour.

'Gunner—' The startled gunner fired – and missed, his shell ploughing up a huge hole behind the Sherman. Now it filled the whole glittering lens of the periscope. 'He's going to ram us!' von Dodenburg yelled, suddenly aware of the Sherman's true intention.

'Up, gunner – a hundred!' he roared next moment.

Sweating frantically, with fluttering, over-excited fingers, the gunner whirled his controls round. Again the long, overhanging 75mm. erupted. In his haste he missed again. The Sherman was whipped from side to side like a toy tank by the blast of the near miss. But still it kept on coming. Von Dodenburg's driver lost his nerve. Without waiting for orders, he thrust home reverse. With a howl the Maybach engine took the strain. 'For God's sake,' von Dodenburg yelled, 'what are you doing?'

The frightened driver was beyond listening. He crashed the Panther through the trees, cracking them like matchsticks, blundering deep into a thicket just as the Sherman flashed by their front in a frightening blur of firing steel. But von Dondenburg's luck was running out. Suddenly the Panther came to an abrupt halt which threw his face against the turret with a mighty thwack. His nose started to bleed and his mouth was suddenly full of the salty taste of blood.

Angrily he shook his head to drive away the blackness that was threatening to overcome him. 'You shitty fool,' he yelled at the driver, whose face was a mass of blood where he, too, had smacked into the controls. 'Get us out of here before the bastards spot the fix we're in!'

Cursing furiously, the driver attempted to start the stalled engine. There was a low harsh groan like the howl of some banshee. Anxiously von Dodenburg shot a glance through the blood-smeared periscope. There were perhaps five Shermans milling around their immediate front, emerging and disappearing into the smoke, obviously trying to find the missing Panther. It would be only a matter of moments before they spotted his predicament. 'Heaven, arse and cloudburst, driver, get the pig started, can't you?' Desperately the sweating driver pressed the starter again. Streams of dark-blue oil smoke began to emerge from the twin exhausts. Still nothing happened. Von Dodenburg swung the periscope round with hands that trembled like leaves in a wind. The Sherman which had tried to ram them had spotted them. Already its gun was beginning to swing round in their direction. 'Stop him, gunner!' von Dodenburg shouted.

This time the blond gunner did not miss. The 75mm. spoke first, and the Sherman reeled on its rear sprockets. A moment later it was a burning shambles of metal and dead men.

Below, the noise from the engine was growing in intensity. 'It's coming, sir, it's coming,' the driver cried wildly over the intercom.

'Yer, like shitty Christmas is coming,' the gunner commented scornfully, as the Mark V started to shake and rattle as if at any moment it would fall apart.

Von Dodenburg clung to the periscope, ashen-faced. If the others spotted them now, they were finished. Rapidly his bloodless lips mumbled the first prayer he had said since he was confirmed in the Prussian Garrison Church in Spandau as a fourteen-year-old. Below, the Maybach was racing furiously, making a hell of a racket. Suddenly there was a series of sharp backfires. White smoke burst from their exhausts. An instant later the 400 h.p. engines broke into full life.

'*We've done it!*' the jubilant driver cried. 'The pig has—'

He never finished the sentence. In that same moment the concentrated fire of five Shermans descended upon the trapped Panther. The driver slumped dead over his shattered controls, the grin of triumph frozen on his face. The gunner slumped back in his leather seat, his face half shot away and lower half of his body, boots and all, thrown to the other end of the turret.

Von Dodenburg tried to fight back the purple blackness that threatened to swamp him. To no avail. Red and white

97

stars exploded in front of his eyes. Blindly he tried to move his hands. He couldn't. 'Driver . . . driver,' he whispered weakly, but his words trailed away to nothing. Next moment his head fell hard against the turret.

'What in a pink arsehole are they, sir?' the black-faced grenadier sergeant, who was minus both boots, gasped, as he stared at the little tracked vehicles, which were dwarfed by the accompanying Shermans.

Gent's frightened gaze took in the little trailers that bounced up and down behind the tracked vehicles as they rolled across the dead khaki-clad bodies scattered everywhere, 'Wasps,' he said, trying to control his voice.

'And what are they when they're shitting well at home, sir?' the sergeant demanded almost angrily.

It was only by a sheer effort of will that Gent was able to bring the words out. 'Flame-throwers!' he gasped.

The sergeant gulped with fear. 'Jesus, Maria, Joseph,' he whispered in his thick Bavarian accent and crossed himself. 'Now we're for the chop.'

Shells from the Shermans began to fall on the weary grenadiers' positions. Gent knew the reason why. The Canadians wanted to keep the defenders' heads down until the mobile flame-throwers were in range. 'Get the mortars!' he yelled urgently to the sergeant.

'There's only one left, sir.'

'Well, get that.'

Doubled low, the sergeant zig-zagged through the shells falling everywhere, and grabbing the two-man mortar that still remained intact, although its crew was long dead, he doubled back to where Gent was waiting.

'Hurry up, let's get the bastard set up,' von der Tanne commanded. 'Before they get within firing distance.'

Working feverishly, and hampered by Gent's crippled hands, they put down the base plate, screwed in the tube and attached it to the tripod, while shells fell all around them.

The first Wasp was within range. It halted. Its gunner

pressed the trigger of his deadly weapon. There was a frightening, hushed intake of air like that of a dragon breathing in. A forked tongue of oil-tinged blue flame shot out of the hose a good hundred metres. In its path the dust shrank back, black and shrivelled. Boulders to its front turned a dull, glowing purple. Even though the boulders were a good fifty metres away from their own position, Gent and the sergeant could feel the horrific heat. It bathed their bodies in sticky sweat immediately, dragging the air from their lungs forcibly.

Gent whipped in the first kilo bomb and ignoring the beads of sweat dripping from his eyebrows, called, 'Ready, Sergeant?'

'Ready, sir.'

A mere hundred and fifty metres away, the Wasp fired again. Again the long tongue of angry flame licked out towards them greedily. The two sweat-soaked Germans ducked hurriedly. Gent felt his camouflaged tunic begin to singe. There was the stench of burning cloth and hair. He fought for breath like a fish stranded on a bank in its death throes.

'Fire!' Gent yelled.

The sergeant twisted the ring. There was a soft plop, followed by a metallic harsh gasp. Next moment the mortar bomb sailed clumsily into the air. Higher and higher. It seemed to Gent, following its progress, that it would never begin its downward flight. Abruptly it changed course, became a hurrying black blur, until it was lost to sight, descending right on the open rear deck of the Wasp. Flame shot two hundred metres into the burning sky. Within seconds the Wasp was a white-hot mess of burning metal.

But there were already others ready to take its place. Now the evil crawling metal monsters were everywhere between the Shermans. At one hundred metres' range they began to spray the Panzer Grenadier positions, firing from left to right systematically.

One by one, Gent's grenadiers were flamed, wreathed in that terrible fire, dropping and writhing in the dust, screaming frantically until they became charred skeletons, shrunk to the size of pygmies. Next to Gent, the sergeant panicked. 'Can't stand anymore . . . can't stand it anymore.' He sprang to his feet, kicking over the mortar that would betray their position, and flinging away his rifle, started to run to the rear. Man after man of the survivors began to follow him.

In vain, Gent tried to stop the rout, his arms outstretched like a schoolteacher trying to catch his pupils at some harmless game in the playground. But the grenadiers had had enough. The terrible all-consuming fire was too much for them. Even their beloved CO could no longer hold them now.

'*Stop . . . stop, for God's sake. Stop, lads . . .*' Gent's desperate plea ended forlornly. All the survivors had gone now, flinging away their helmets and weapons in their haste to escape that terrible fire. He was alone with the dead. Slowly, warily, the remaining Wasps began to close on the heap of smoking ruins that had once been the key village of Cintheaux.

Gent gulped with fear. What was he to do? He glanced down. His white gloves had gone, sucked off by that terrible flame, to reveal the horrible, pink, crooked claws which had once been hands that he had concealed beneath them. 'My God,' he cried aloud to the burning unresponsive sky, 'why . . . *Why?*'

The sight of his own terrible disfigurement finally broke Captain von der Tanne. After five years of total war, his nerve went at last.

Clutching the absurd swagger stick in his red claws, his breeches blackened and ripped, only one of his precious silver spurs left on his muddy riding boots, he charged towards the advancing Wasps, yelling obscenities.

A bored Canadian corporal, chewing gum with practised routine, pressed the trigger of his deadly weapon. Captain von der Tanne, scion of a family which had fought for the Great Elector, Old Fritz, the First Wilhelm and the Second, disappeared in a sudden puff of violet flame. All they ever found afterwards was one heat-buckled silver spur. As the Canadian trooper who found it the next day remarked, 'Jeez, I didn't know the Krauts was still using cavalry . . .'

Von Dodenburg's eyes fluttered, opened, closed again. Someone forced something metallic between his gritted teeth. He was forced to swallow the liquid. A moment later he was coughing and spluttering, his eyes filled with tears at the fiery taste. 'What . . . what . . . ?'

'All right, sir,' a well-remembered rough voice said from what seemed far away. 'All right, all right . . .'

Von Dodenburg opened his eyes.

Schulze was looking down at him, his blackened face full of concern. Behind him Matz stared down at the pale-faced officer, his black eyes anxious. 'What happened?' he asked weakly. 'Why are you . . . here . . . ?'

'Your Panther bought it, sir. Two others as well. Three of mine. I thought it best to bug out. There was no holding them—'

'And Cintheaux?' Von Dodenburg struggled free of Schulze's big brawny arm and raised himself.

'Look for yourself, sir,' Matz said, and indicated down below. The hamlet was covered with a thick rolling cloud of yellow smoke. Von Dodenburg looked at it uncomprehendingly. 'What happened?' he asked, after what seemed a long time.

Matz drew a dirty forefinger under his throat. 'Curtains,' he said.

'Yessir. They're all dead, except a couple of dozen who hoofed it,' Schulze agreed. 'The Canadians used shitting flamethrowers. Those young wet-tails of Captain von der Tanne didn't stand a chance.'

'And the Captain?'

'Bought it too. He was last seen attacking the whole Canadian Army on his lonesome.'

Von Dodenburg let his head hang. 'Oh, my God,' he moaned. 'What is left of my poor regiment?'

'Not very much, sir,' Schulze said slowly. 'What you can

see – a dozen Panthers and the handful of Panzer Grenadiers who managed to beat it from the village before it got the chop.' He shrugged. 'Perhaps fifty at the most. And they're buggered to the world, the poor young shits.'

Weakly von Dodenburg stared at the handful of survivors, outlined a stark weary black against the setting sun. The well-remembered bold urgency had gone from their faces and they seemed to have aged overnight. Even in his weakened state, he realized that they were almost at the end of their tether. He sank back again and gratefully accepted another sip of the fierce apple brandy that Schulze offered him. 'What are we going to do?' he asked, as if speaking to himself.

Schulze answered the question for him. Rubbing a big paw across his blackened unshaven chin and staring at the desolate battle-shattered horizon, he said, 'From now on, sir, there's only one thing left to do if we're gonna save what's left of Wotan.'

'And what's that?'

There was a sudden anger in the big Hamburger's voice. 'It's gonna be, now – *march or croak* . . .'

THE LONG RETREAT

'Should the new weapons in which you place so much hope . . . not bring success – then, my Führer, make up your mind to end the war. The German people have suffered so unspeakably that it is time to bring the horror to a close.'

FM von Kluge to Adolf Hitler in his suicide note, Aug. 18th, 1944.

ONE

Field Marshal von Kluge was alone in the gloomy study at the Chateau de la Roche Guyon, bent over the big map, when General Blumentritt entered to say his good-byes. He seemed unaware of the other officer's presence, and it was only after Blumentritt had cleared his throat loudly several times that the former Commander-in-Chief, West, turned and became aware of the other man. 'Ah, it's you, my dear Blumentritt,' he said wearily, his once plump, healthy face, drawn and pinched.

'I came to wish you good-bye – *and* good luck, Field Marshal,' Blumentritt said. He knew that the new Commander-in-Chief, West, Field Marshal Model, had handed the beaten von Kluge a personal letter from the Führer himself, and that it instructed his former Chief to report forthwith the Führer HQ. That could mean only one thing.

'Thank you, Blumentritt, it is very kind of you,' von Kluge answered. 'You are the only one. The rest . . .' He shrugged carelessly. 'I should imagine that Field Marshal Model has perhaps given them no time to do so.'

'Probably, sir,' Blumentritt agreed loyally. But with the increasing volume of artillery fire in the distance, he knew most of the staff were packing, ready for the race back to Germany.

Sadly, the man who had been once known throughout the army as 'Clever Hans'[1] tapped the map with his pencil. 'Here, at Avranches, all my military reputation went. Do you remember the book old Moltke wrote which saved the honour of his opponent Benedek?'[2]

Blumentritt nodded.

'Well, there is no Moltke for me.'

'But, Field Marshal, you must not take it so seriously. The overwhelming air superiority of the enemy. Their armour—'

Von Kluge held up his hand for the other man to stop. 'Thank you, Blumentritt, but I know it's all up with me. Model is preparing now the order for the army to withdraw from France and I must be prepared, too, to take the consequences for that defeat.' He held out his hand and took Blumentritt's. 'Now, my dear Blumentritt, you must go and do your duty as I must do mine. Good-bye.'

'Good-bye, sir.'

Blumentritt was not an emotional man, but he could hardly keep back the tears at the utterly tragic look on his former Chief's face. Without another word, he turned and went out, closing the study door softly behind him. Somehow he knew he would never see 'Clever Hans' again.

Wearily, very wearily, von Kluge walked over to the antique table at the end of the gloomy study, and taking out pen and paper, began to write the letter to the Führer that he had been thinking about all day, ever since Model had arrived with the order dismissing him from his command.

It was a long letter, in which he still tried to defend his conduct of operations in the West, although he knew it no longer mattered; he was finished. But in the end, his true feelings came through, after years of toadying to the monster who had run the affairs of the Reich these last terrible

[1] A play on his name, Hans von Kluge, '*klug*' meaning in English 'clever'.
[2] Reference to Prussian General von Moltke's chivalry in protecting the reputation of his defeated Austrian opponent, Gen. Benedek after the Battle of Sadowa in 1866.

war years. Dipping his pen time and time again in the almost empty inkwell, he wrote, 'Should the new weapons in which you place so much hope, especially those of the air force, not bring success – then, my Führer, make up your mind to end the war. The German people have suffered so unspeakably that it is time to bring the horror to a close. I have steadfastly stood in awe of your greatness, your bearing in this gigantic struggle, and your iron will. If Fate is stronger than your will and your genius, that is Destiny. You have made an honourable and tremendous fight. History will testify this for you. Show now that greatness that will be necessary if it comes to the point of ending a struggle which has become hopeless. I depart—' he hesitated about completing the fateful word, but in the end he did —'from you, my Führer, having stood closer to you in spirit than you perhaps dreamed, in the consciousness of having done my duty to the utmost.' Fully conscious that he was now deciding his own fate, he added his signature to the long letter, 'Hans von Kluge.'

Just before midday, the Field Marshal ordered his chauffeur to stop the big, six-wheeled command car. Before them on the dead straight white road lay the towering, grim heights of Verdun, where he had fought in his youth in another war. 'We shall lunch here, Tangermann,' he ordered his aide.

Obediently Tangermann and the chauffeur spread a plaid rug under a group of convenient, dusty trees and began to eat their haversack rations.

Von Kluge sat alone, a little aside from the other two, leaving untouched the sandwiches spread out in front of him. Tangermann, mouth full of bread and sausage, looked across at his chief curiously. What was going on in the Old Man's mind? he asked himself.

Von Kluge caught the look. 'Prepare everything for departure in a quarter of an hour,' he commanded, with just a trace of his old cold haughtiness, which had made him so feared among his subordinates at the height of his power.

'*Jawohl, Herr Generalfeldmarschall*,' Tangermann snapped, and concentrated on his sandwich.

Von Kluge looked up at the heights which had seen the greatest blood-letting in all history and wished somehow he had died there nearly a quarter of a century earlier. It would have been a more honourable way to go, death in battle, dying for one's country. But that fate was not to be his. He must take a more ignoble way out, but at least he would not end it all like von Paulus.[1] What had the Führer said at the time? 'A German Field Marshal does not surrender.' He had applauded those sentiments at the time. Now he must live up to them.

Slowly he reached in the pocket of his tunic and stared down at the little phial which had accompanied him everywhere since the start of the Russian campaign in 1941. How curious, he thought, that such a little thing could mean the end of it all – over three decades in the service of one's country: the Kaiser, the Republic and then Adolf Hitler, who he had so admired for taking Germany out of the trough of despair after Versailles. '*Such a little thing*,' he whispered to himself, '*such a little thing*.' Abruptly he made his decision. He put the phial between his false teeth and bit hard. Immediately the bitter-tasting poison flooded his mouth, ran, burning unbearably, down his throat into his stomach, ripping and tearing away the sensitive membranes as it went. He fell to the dusty earth, writhing back and forth in agony, the froth gathering at once at his suddenly blue lips.

'*Herr Generalfeldmarschall!*' Tangermann cried in alarm, dropping his sandwich and springing to his feet, 'What have you done?'

But there was no answer. Abruptly the Field Marshal's spine arched like a bow, his hands clawing the air, as if he were trying to climb some invisible ladder. Next instant, the man who had nearly captured Moscow, and who had been defeated by a group of elderly, shabby boffins in a

[1] FM von Paulus, who had surrendered with his 6th Army to the Russians at Stalingrad in 1943.

remote English country house, fell back dead. It was exactly 3.20 on the afternoon of August 18th, 1944, and the German army in the West was in full retreat!

TWO

Vehicles were piling up everywhere, as somewhere up ahead the *Jabos* came swooping down yet again to attack targets the like of which they had not seen in five years of war. Staff cars full of frightened senior officers, and laden with the loot of four years of Occupation, honked their horns angrily and attempted to fight their way through the impossible jam. At the side of the blocked highway leading east, tired, worn, dusty gunners were abandoning their 88's, pulling out the firing pins and breaking them across the rocks, or throwing a couple of stick grenades down their muzzles. The *Jabos* came zooming in. The crews of some rear-line workshops abandoned their vehicles in panic, streaming out to the fields on either side the road, which were already littered with dead men and fat bloated dead cows, their hooves sticking up into the air so that they looked like tethered barrage-balloons.

Rockets flashed, cannons chattered. Workshop trucks, tank transporters, went up in flames. A goulash cannon was hit. Boiling hot giddi-up soup[1] scalded the hidden mechanics behind the hedges, and in their overwhelming fear they did not realize just how badly burnt they were. The *Jabos* had a field day. Even the poorest gunner among the pilots could not miss. The enemy soft vehicles were packed four abreast on the highway east. The *Jabos* threw everything they had at the jammed column – rockets, bullets, cannon-shells, bombs. There were even those who slowed down to near stalling speed to drop grenades out of their cockpits at the halted Germans, like pilots fighting at the front in 1914, when aerial warfare was in its infancy.

[1] Wotan's name for horsemeat soup.

Lathes, electric drills, automatic welders, spare parts by the hundred flew through the air, flattening the hedges on both sides, killing everyone who crouched in their path.

'Great balls of flying crap!' Schulze, in the lead tank, cried in awe. 'They'll be throwing the kitchen sink at us next!' He ducked the next instant, as a kitchen sink from some mobile cookhouse whizzed by his big head.

This day, however, Colonel von Dodenburg, leading what was left of Wotan, had no time for Schulze's humour. Now it was *suave qui peut* – every man for himself – and he was determined to save his men. He felt he owed that to those who had already died so futilely. The fate of the frightened base stallions of the workshop unit who had spent four cushy years in France did not concern him.

'Matz,' he commanded harshly above the racket, 'advance! Cut through the bastards if they don't get out of the way!'

Matz needed no urging. 'With the greatest of pleasure, sir,' he answered gleefully. Pressing his foot down hard on the accelerator and engaging first gear, he started towards the jam of burning vehicles. Frightened workshop officers emerged from the ditches where they had been hiding when they saw his intention, waving their arms urgently and trying to stop him.

Matz pushed on. Like all front-line swine he hated the base stallions who probably hadn't heard a shot fired in anger since 1940. Cursing furiously, officers sprang out of the path of the 40-ton monster just in time. An elderly fat captain, with the brick-red face and thickened nose of a heavy drinker, failed to move in time. The tank struck him. He disappeared under its tracks, screaming in agony. The Panther pressed him flat into the dust of the road, as if his body had been made of cardboard.

Von Dodenburg, standing anxiously on the turret, did not even look back. Schulze did. 'He makes a very neat corpse,' he remarked, almost to himself. 'Be easy to pack him up and send him home like that.'

Behind them, there was the frightened cry 'Shermans!'

everywhere. Cooks, quartermasters, sky-pilots, clerks – the whole rabble of the rear echelon – who had never expected to face up to anything like this, fled in panicked confusion. Staff officers, their chateaux, champagne and classy chats about the cosmos forgotten now, ran amok. Some placed their automatics melodramatically in their mouths, gagging at the awful taste of the oil, and blew themselves to eternity. Others sold all they possessed for a shabby suit of French civilian clothes and made a dive for the homes of their French girl-friends. A few even went into the slit trenches and tried to hold the enemy back. But only a few.

The front had broken down completely. On the same day that Field Marshal Model ordered the withdrawal from France, what was left of Hausser's Seventh Army and the 5th Panzer Army were caught in the trap created when the Americans and the Poles linked up at Falaise. Nearly 100,000 men – the shattered remnants of fifteen divisions – were herded together in a pocket, twenty-two miles wide and eleven miles deep.

Without a pause, the fighter-bombers of the U.S. Army Air Corps and the RAF bombed and strafed them, knowing they would never have a chance like this again: 100,000 men, without any form of aerial defence or flak. Some formations simply disintegrated. Others surrendered *en masse* – if they could. Most milled around, sick with despair, worn out by a month of constant bombing and strafing, taking whatever cover they could find in the wasted, blackened countryside, waiting for the inevitable end.

But there were others, a few others, who were determined to fight their way out through the narrow gap left between Saint-Lambert and Chambois, and one of those few was SS Assault Regiment Wotan.

On the afternoon of 19th August, the sky about them mercilessly burning, without a cloud to offer any cover from the enemy *Jabos*, Colonel von Dodenburg finally found Colonel-General Paul Hausser's HQ and for the first time in nearly a week, learned something of the true situation within the Falaise pocket.

Hausser and his staff, all as ragged, dusty and dirty as the thin, haggard SS officer himself, were crouched under the pathetic cover of an apple orchard when the Panthers rolled to a stop. There was an immediate panic at the sight of the tanks. 'They'll attract the *Jabos*!' staff officers cried in alarm. 'For God's sake, Colonel, get the hell out of here! You want to have us all killed, man?'

In the end, a weary 'Papa' Hausser himself had to step in and sort the situation out. The Panzers could remain, but they had to be camouflaged and driven at once deep into the apple trees.

Thus, while his weary men sweated at Schulze's orders, stumbling back and forth like sleepwalkers to bring branches to drape above their tanks, von Dodenburg crouched at Hausser's feet to listen to the Colonel-General's plan with the rest of those who wanted to break out.

'There is no time to work out a careful plan, gentlemen,' Hausser said wearily. 'The situation is too grave for any kind of general-staff work. Everything now must be improvised, done at the last minute with the bits and pieces of broken formations that are still left to us.' He drew a rough line in the dust at his feet with a twig. 'Chambois! At dawn, what is left of the SS Bodyguard Division will attack here with its armour. At the same time, the 3rd Parachute Division, which will have got into position during the darkness, will attack here – at St Lambert. Those will be our two escape routes, to be held by the two divisions concerned as long as they can. You gentlemen can select the one most suitable to your particular formation. Naturally, once the enemy becomes aware of our intentions at Chambois and St Lambert, they will throw in all the weight they have to block the gaps. But that is the chance we must take if we are going to save anything from this unholy mess. Gentlemen, I would like to wish you all the best—'

General Hausser never finished his last sentence. In that same instant as the officers rose to depart to their own formations, there was an unholy howl as the *Jabos* came diving down, attracted by the vehicles hidden in the trees. Cannon chattered. 20mm. came flashing redly through the trees. Wildly the generals and their staffs dived for cover. But not all of them were swift enough. Colonel von Gersdorf, Hausser's Chief of Staff, was hit. Hausser, too, staggered weakly against a tree, wounded in the face. And then the *Jabos* were gone, leaving a smoking trail of death and destruction behind them.

Hausser waved back the officers who rushed forward from their cover to help him. 'It is of no consequence, gentlemen,' he said weakly. 'You must return to what is left of your units at once while there is still time.' He stared around at their anxious white faces with his one eye, until it rested upon von Dodenburg's harshly handsome features, so that the young colonel could not help thinking that the army commander's words were addressed specifically at him. 'Ensure that you get as many men out as possible. They are the ones who want to fight – the rest are rabble. And our beloved Fatherland will have need of fighters in the terrible months to come.'

As the fresh howl of engines from the west indicated that another wave of dive-bombers were on their way, Colonel-General Hausser touched his hand to his peaked cap with the fading, tarnished death's-head of the once proud Armed SS which he had created. 'Gentlemen,' he said sadly, as if he were seeing them for the last time, 'I salute you.'

And then they were all running, generals and lieutenants, to their vehicles, in a mad, undignified scramble to get away before the *Jabos* swamped them with fire yet again.

THREE

It was the constant, persistent sledgehammer of the enemy shells smashing into the packed ranks of the survivors, which brought terror to their souls. Time and time again the shells struck home. Towering pillars of oily black smoke rose incessantly, after the gas tank of yet another vehicle was hit. Dump after dump of ammunition exploded with a frightening crump, sending the riderless horses of the abandoned artillery stampeding, foam at their muzzles, through the packed ranks of the men waiting impatiently to cross the River Dives at St Lambert, once it was finally dark.

But the blood-red August sun obstinately refused to go down. The slit trenches and foxholes filled to overflowing with the freshly wounded and the dying. As for the living, the flesh around their blood-scummed, cracked lips quivered at every fresh detonation and their eyes were covered with a hot wet sheen, as if they were close to tears and raging hysteria.

The tremendous pounding from all sides continued. Young men became old. Old men went mad. But, mad and old, the only sounds they uttered, their voices unheard in that murderous bombardment, were cries of agony and prayers to a God who had long abandoned them. The rest was merely an animal whimpering.

Von Dodenburg, crouching in the protection of his battered Panther, its sides bullet-pocked and shrapnel-scarred so that it looked as if it suffered from some loathsome skin disease, shook his fist at the obstinate ball of the sun and cried: 'For God's sake – *go down, damn you!*'

Then finally the killing sun started to vanish over the horizon, and as if by magic the artillery bombardment ceased. Von Dodenburg rose from his hiding-place. All around him, his troopers, too, were getting to their feet, looking at each as if in wonder that they were still alive after the slaughter of that long terrible day. The colonel drank deeply of the last of the brackish water in his canteen and then tossed it away to join the rest of the equipment abandoned by the thousands of men who had come this way. 'Schulze and Matz,' he commanded, 'ensure that the tanks are carefully sabotaged.'

'Already done, sir,' Matz said, with some of his old cheerfulness.

'Yessir,' Schulze chimed in. 'Anyone who tries to start these babies is gonna get an awful bad case of piles. We attached four grenades to each starter.' He slapped the command Panther's metal side affectionately. 'Gonna be hard to get used to being a stubble-hopper again, without our iron horses.'

'Well, you were the one who said it was going to be march or croak from now on, Schulze. March on your flat feet you will—'

'Crap, said the king, and a thousand assholes bent and took the strain, for in those days the word of the king was law,' Schulze, who was no respecter of persons, commented. 'March I shitting well will have to do.'

'All ready, men,' von Dodenburg cried, raising his voice so that the weary sweating troopers hidden everywhere in the bushes could hear. 'The Paras will be going in soon. On your feet. We'll follow.'

'And I'll have the eggs off anybody who makes a noise – with a blunt razorblade – *slowly*,' Schulze threatened. 'Now, make dust.'

Von Dodenburg looked at his men's faces. They were blank, but the troopers' twitching lips and dilated eyes revealed, all too clearly, the hell they had been through. This night, if anything went wrong, they would stampede like all the rest who were going to attempt the break-through behind the Paras at the river. He said a silent prayer that nothing would go wrong and commanded 'Forward!' The break-out attempt had begun.

Von Dodenburg crouched in the high willows at the edge of the Dives. Next to him some poor stubble-hopper had been cut in half by a shell, an apparently endless length of intestine stretching from the massive wound. Von Dodenburg forced himself to look away and view the river, gleaming silver in the faint moonlight.

It was not very big, perhaps four metres broad and a couple of metres deep. It wouldn't be difficult to cross, as long as they were not spotted by the enemy artillery, which would alert the Canadians, already dug in on either side of the narrow escape gap. Everything depended on the Paras silencing the Canadian troops closest to the gap on the other side.

Down at the water's edge, he heard the Paratroop CO, in the airborne's characteristic rimless helmet, give his last orders. Carefully, very carefully, the Paras started to wade into the stream. To von Dodenburg, they seemed to make a hell of a noise, but he reasoned that his nerves were on edge. In all probability, the Canadians were already fast asleep, confident that they had the Germans safely tied up in the trap.

Now the point was halfway across. Von Dodenburg, and the men hiding in the willows all around him, tensed. Soon they would reach the other side. Was the enemy lying in wait for them?

The Para CO stumped out of the water, and reaching up for a hold, started to climb the muddy bank. Next to von Dodenburg, Schulze whispered, 'Arse and soul, sir, this waiting really puts the wind up yer.'

Von Dodenburg nodded his agreement grimly.

The Para CO crouched on the opposite bank. Von Dodenburg could see him outlined quite clearly against the silver sheen of the moon. Could the Canadians, too? Apparently not. After a moment the Para placed his hand, fingers outstretched, on the top of his helmet. It was the infantry signal for 'rally on me'. Instantly, the Paras started to struggle out of the water, up the bank, disappearing to left and right on either side to cover the flanks.

Von Dodenburg pulled out his pistol. Next to him, Matz did the same with his knife, and Schulze drew a grenade out of his boot. 'Ready to move out!' von Dodenburg commanded. 'Weapons ready.' Then, 'Follow me, Wotan.'

Eagerly the troopers flooded after him down the muddy bank and waded into the river. Still all was silence on the other side. Presumably the Paras had done a good job of silencing the Canadian outposts nearest to the gap. They were nearly across now. Behind him von Dodenburg could hear the next group of escapees begin to enter the water. Now he began to hope that they would get through without being detected, after all. But that was not to be.

There was a sudden clatter of horses' hooves. A loud challenge. A frightened voice cried, 'I tell you, I have priority. I am General Kurtz. I must join my command!'

'Stop the crazy fool!' someone cried.

But the panic-stricken general was not to be stopped. He urged his horse into the water. It made a tremendous noise as it galloped deep into the river, scattering startled soldiers on both sides.

'Who goes there?' came the cry in English. It was followed a moment later by, 'Christ, the Kraut bastards are trying to break out! *Stand to . . . Stand to, everybody!*'

Von Dodenburg hesitated no longer. 'At the double!' he yelled, and dived for the far bank. Flares hissed into the sky on all sides, bathing the escapees in their sickly icy light. Machine-guns started to chatter. Glowing tracer scythed across the surface of the water. The massacre of the escapees had begun.

As the general was flung off his panicked horse by the first vicious burst of m.g. fire, von Dodenburg cried, 'Wotan, follow me!'

The men streamed out of the water, firing from the hip as they did so. They burst through a hedge. The thorns tore at von Dodenburg's uniform and flesh. He didn't notice it. There could be no stopping now. Small-arms fire was coming in from all sides. A confused mess of red and white tracer hissed angrily through the darkness, like lethal fireflies.

Behind them, the first shells were beginning to fall on the river crossing. Tanks went up in flames. Horse-drawn artillery pieces exploded, shattering horse-flesh everywhere. Men screamed and sank below the water, never to reappear. Swiftly the Dives began to block with dead and dying men. The massacre was in full swing.

Pistol in hand, von Dodenburg ran on. He stumbled into a Canadian outpost. His pistol cracked. A surprised

Canadian went down. Behind him, Schulze lobbed a grenade into another group of enemy soldiers rushing the CO. They disintegrated. Von Dodenburg felt the blast. It slapped him across the face, followed, a moment later, by a rain of blood. But he had no time to wipe it off. The Canadians were everywhere on the height.

The high shape of a Sherman loomed up out of the darkness. Matz didn't hesitate. In spite of his one leg, he was up on the turret like a monkey. His knife flashed in the darkness. There was a shrill, almost feminine scream. And another. In an instant he had set the tank in motion, heading for the Canadians chasing them up the height. With its crew of dead men, it trundled straight into them, throwing them to left and right.

The sweat was pouring down von Dodenburg's face. His lungs were threatening to burst at any moment and he felt he must drop soon. But he forced his body on mercilessly. To stop now would mean death.

They blundered into an enemy machine-gun pit. Before the startled Canadians could open fire, they were slaughtered where they crouched. Some infantry, covering the pit, rushed the escapees with fixed bayonets. It was the last thing they did. Schulze's machine-pistol scythed them down. And then they were through the Canadian line and running and tumbling down the other side of the height, laughing and screaming crazily like a bunch of school-kids released from school at the start of a long summer vacation, while behind them the Massacre of the River Dives came to its final bloody end.

What followed was a strange night, full of abrupt alarms and sudden frights. On all sides there was the vicious snap and crackle of small-arms fire. Tracer hissed hotly through the darkness. Flares sailed into the air, time and time again. There were cries in half a dozen languages. More than once they heard German. But von Dodenburg did not stop. He knew that the only way they were going to escape the débâcle in France was to rely on themselves. Wotan would go it alone. Twice they ran into Polish positions and silenced them with knife, spade and club. Once they got caught in a barbed-wire entanglement, which seemed to stretch for metres both left and right, and which made von Dodenburg despair of ever getting through it. But they did in the end – at the cost of much blood and flesh.

The night hours passed in sweating, frightened anxiety. Some of the younger troopers, exhausted, or weak from the lack of blood, began to lag behind. Von Dodenburg urged them on with threats and promises. By dawn, he, Schulze and Matz were carrying three weapons apiece and were bringing up the rear of the column, pistols drawn, threatening to shoot anyone who dropped out.

Just after dawn they passed the first German tank, a knocked-out Mark IV, but its crew were still there, dug in around a machine-gun in a ditch.

'Who are you?' von Dodenburg called.

'Von Luttwitz's division, sir,' one of the scared lonely Panzermen called back. 'Stuck out here in the arse-hole of the world. We're the rearguard.'

'Tough shit,' Schulze said contemptuously, noting the fear and self-pity in the man's voice. 'But don't worry sonny, I'll send you a nice wish-you-were-here card from Berlin.'

'Up yours!'

'And your mother's,' Schulze answered routinely, and stamped on.

Now they started to pass through the lines of the Panzer Division commanded by General von Luttwitz, if the hastily erected road-blocks and dug-in handful of tanks could be called a line. By nine o'clock the rash of signs everywhere and the increasing volume of dusty DRs carrying despatches and VW jeeps bearing weary, but self-important, staff officers, indicated they were approaching an HQ.

Von Dodenburg halted his weary men. They stumbled to a stop. He looked at their sweat-lathered, blacked faces. Some of them had their eyes closed, as if they were sleeping on their feet. Others were swaying violently, staying upright only by an effort of will. His red-rimmed eyes glowed with tired pride. There was nothing like them in the whole world. They were the best. Deliberately harshening his voice, he cried suddenly, 'Sergeant-Major Schulze, get those men formed up into ranks – *at once*, do you hear?'

Across the way, at their farmhouse HQ, von Luttwitz's staff officers, working feverishly over the maps to plan the route back to the Reich, turned, startled by the noise.

'All right, you shower of shitters,' Schulze snarled, 'you heard what the Colonel said.' He slung the rifle back at the soldier for whom he had been carrying it most of the night and nearly knocked him off his feet. 'Form up. What do you think this is – a boarding school for the daughters of high-born crapping ladies? No, this is the Wotan! Now, are you gonna make me wait much longer?'

Wearily, very wearily, the survivors of the break-out formed up into four ranks. Schulze ordered them to slope arms, and as formally as if he were back on some peace-time training ground, reported to a waiting von Dodenburg that the regiment was ready to move off. Von Dodenburg thanked him politely and then, with his handsome ema-ciated face set in a proud look, he cried, 'SS Assault Re-giment Wotan forward *march!*'

While the assembled Panzermen gaped at them, as if they were mad, the last survivors of Wotan began to limp pain-fully after their CO, the blood still dripping from their wounds, some of them barefoot, others virtually naked where the river and the bushes had ripped off their uni-forms, moving by sheer will-power, but with their young battle-hardened faces set, as if they could continue for ever.

At the window of his HQ, gross, red-faced General von Luttwitz screwed in his monocle more firmly. '*SS Wotan, meine Herren,*' he announced. '*Those damned, thrice-damned, brave SS bastards have made it!*' Gently he raised his fat pudgy hand to his head, as if in salute . . .

FOUR

'Well, you big rogue, what did you get?'

Schulze grinned at his CO. 'It's gonna be like the feeding of the five thousand, sir,' he announced, tossing the five looted loaves at the starving troopers. 'One mule dick,' he said, throwing a long sausage after the bread. 'A tin of monkey grease.' Margarine followed. 'Some putty.' A slab of soft cheese whizzed through the air. 'And my little crippled friend, here, has managed to organize some nigger sweat.' He gestured at Matz, red-faced and laden down under two steaming cans of coffee, which he had just stolen from the Quartermaster section.

'And the train?' von Dodenburg asked anxiously, as the starving young troopers tore into the food, the first they had had in the last twenty-four hours of the crazy retreat through the burning-hot French countryside. He stared across the packed square of Rouen's main station, while Schulze fished in his pocket for the looted cigars. Most of the field-greys were completely worn-out. They squatted on the kerbs in the burning heat, heads sunk between their knees in utter weariness. Others stood around staring blankly and apathetically into nothing, while ragged, filthy officers struggled through the evil-smelling crowd of disorganized soldiery, discussing the abysmal situation in low, tense voices. Von Dodenburg knew that it would take the appearance of one lone enemy tank, and the whole miserable rabble would surrender there and then. They were beaten. Rouen was the end of the road for the many thousands packed into the square, waiting for trains that never came.

Schulze puffed greedily at the cigar, and then with a flourish, handed it to his CO. 'There's a train due in in one hour, sir,' he said, keeping his voice low, knowing that if the news leaked out there would be a panic-stricken rush to get onto the platform. 'I got it from the chief kitchen-bull. He did his training with me in Wittlich in '39.[1] Got

[1] See *SS Panzer Battalion* for further details.

his ballocks shot off in Russia, so they made him a kitchen-bull as a sort of consolation prize. If he can't ferk, they said, at least he could feed his face as much as he—'

'Get on with it.'

'Well, sir, he said that he had been ordered to report with one kitchen crew to the back of the station, where the goods yard is – opposite the church. They've already got the seriously wounded there and they're gonna offload the slit—'

'Women?' von Dodenburg demanded sharply.

'Yessir, the train is being reserved for essential personnel, meaning – with permission – senior officers who are creaming their skivvies in case the Tommies bag them, the wounded, and grey mice.'

'That bunch of officers' mattresses,' Matz said scornfully, using the normal description for the 'grey mice', the female auxiliaries of the German Army. 'The only work they ever did was on their backs.'

'They've got to protect the flower of German womanhood from the rapacious Frogs, haven't they?' Schulze said pompously. 'You wouldn't like some Frog sticking his filthy Frog thing into a girl who could be yer sister, would you, Matzi?'

'If you knew what my sister looked like,' Matz said sourly, 'yer'd know she'd be glad to get a Chink's dong between—' The remainder of his words were drowned by the honking of a horn. They spun round. A small motor-bus had been halted by the throng, and in spite of the furious honking of its red-faced, frightened army driver, it could proceed no further. Now its passengers were descending, to a sudden hail of insults and obscene gestures from the soldiers, their weariness vanished for a few moments.

'Slit – real female slit.' Schulze exclaimed, letting the cigar fall from his open mouth.

Women were streaming out of the bus, each carrying a bulging briefcase, and attempting a defiant swing of the buttocks, as they started to push their way through the jeering throng.

Most of them were old and fat, with dyed frizzy hair, and too-tight, too-short silken dresses, though a few were so skinny and sallow-cheeked in spite of the liberal application of rouge to their consumptive features that von Dodenburg doubted they would survive the month. A big blonde of forty-five or so, with a massive bosom that threatened to pop out of her blouse at any moment, and a look on her face that said she'd seen this kind of thing before and probably would again, pushed a jeering oaf of an artillery-man out of the way, who was trying to thrust his big paw into her blouse, and growled, 'Bugger off, Ferdy before your dong falls off!' She raised her middle finger contemptuously as a parting gesture, and disappeared into the crowd.

'Naturally,' Matz sneered, 'they'll be going on the train too, the whole shitting knocking-shop of 'em, to keep the gentlemen officers from getting bored!'

'You mean they . . . they belong to a brothel, Matz?' von Dodenburg asked incredulously.

'Yessir, that's the famous Red-Rimmed Rosie, and I don't suppose I need to tell you how she got that particular name, sir. Everybody used to go to her – er – establishment when they were on leave in Rouen. I nearly had a go myself once, when I had a forty-eight. But I took one look at Red-Rimmed, and, of course, I knew of her complaint,' he added somewhat mysteriously, 'and I thought I'd pass her up.'

'Yer, you with that little dingle of yourn would,' Schulze sneered. 'So that's Red-Rimmed Rosie, is it? I've heard of her.' Schulze sucked at his teeth thoughtfully. 'A knocking shop on wheels, eh?' he said, as if to himself. 'A very attractive proposition indeed. But those little women are going to have to venture into the unknown without the protection of some strong loving man. It is not a prospect that any honest German soldier can view with ease.'

'What the devil are you babbling on about, Schulze?' von Dodenburg demanded.

'Well, sir, would you agree that Wotan is about buggered?'

'I would.'

'And would you also agree that if we don't get out of Rouen soon, we're going to end up in the bag?'

'Yes,' von Dodenburg said wearily, 'I would agree to that statement, too.'

'And finally would you agree that that there Red-Rimmed Rosie possesses a very strong personality, and that with that string of trotters on two legs she runs she has a very powerful weapon in her hands vis-à-vis the RTO,[1] who might well not be disinclined to cut himself off one last piece of female ass before he wanders off into the Tommy cage, and has to change over to brown cake—'

'In three devils' name, Schulze,' von Dodenburg roared impatiently, 'get on with it!'

'Well, sir, this is what Mrs Schulze's handsome son is thinking . . .' Swiftly he explained his plan.

Von Dodenburg clapped his hand to his temple when Schulze had finished, and groaned, 'Great crap on the Christmas Tree! Now you want to turn Wotan into a bunch of pimps, Schulze!'

'It whacks being a corpse any day, sir,' Schulze said cheerfully, and without another word disappeared into the throng to carry out his self-appointed task.

FIVE

With a great clattering of wheels, a rusty squeaking of brakes, and a huge cloud of steam, the long camouflaged train bearing the usual legend on its side 'Wheels run for Victory', came to a halt in the siding. For one long moment nothing happened, as if the hundreds waiting to board the train could not believe the evidence of their own eyes – that the long promised rescue train had really arrived.

[1] Railway Transport Officer.

Abruptly the platform came to life. The 'grey mice' who had been pressed into service as stretcher-bearers began carrying the seriously wounded through the steam towards the white-painted coaches to the front, with their enormous red-cross markings. Senior officers followed, surging forward, their dignity forgotten now, as they jostled and cursed each other in their eagerness to get aboard. Here and there the chaindogs were forced to use their rifle butts to drive the senior officers apart. Over the loudspeakers, the metallic voice of an agreeably surprised and pleasantly weary RTO called, 'Gentlemen, I beg you, please. There is room for everyone with the special pass. *Please!*'

Von Dodenburg tore his contemptuous gaze from the unpleasant sight, and said to Schulze who crouched beside him behind the package cases, 'Now what? There are military police everywhere.'

Schulze tapped the side of his big nose cunningly. 'Never fear, sir. They're gonna to have other problems on their hands in a minute.' He glanced down at his watch. 'The train'll leave in exactly five minutes. In exactly four minutes time, Matz is going to boff the RTO over his lecherous turnip and shout over the loudspeakers that there is a train here. Can you imagine what's going to happen out there on the square?'

'I can indeed. Then what?'

'We run like hell to where she's standing, over there.' He indicated the spot where the blonde Red-Rimmed Rosie was guarding the door to her girls' coach with a club clutched in her mighty, beringed fist. 'The chaindogs will be busy with the mob. The driver'll shit his pants and take off.' He beamed at the CO. 'And Wotan will be heading for Germany, home, and beauty in the comfort and company of a group of beautiful ladies.'

Von Dodenburg struck his forehead in mock anguish. 'Pimping, occupation of a reserved train, and now striking an RTO,' he groaned. 'God only knows, Schulze, you'll land me before a firing squad yet!'

Pleasurably, the RTO sniffed at the delicate perfume coming from the pair of black silk panties which Rosie had given him – 'to console me in the lonely nights in the camp,' he had pleaded, with much significant rolling of his eyes – and thought of that delicious five minutes he had spent with the whorehouse madame up against the wall of his cubicle. Deep in lascivious thoughts, he did not hear the soft footfall behind him until it was too late. Matz's club struck directly on the back of his bald skull and he pitched forward soundlessly onto his desk, his long nose buried into the fragrant crotch of Rosie's black panties.

Matz grabbed the mike. 'Here's the main station RTO,' he announced in his best Prussian-officer's voice, listening to the metallic echo bounce back and forth along the walls of the square. 'Pay attention to the following message. A troop train will be arriving at the goods station bound for the Reich in exactly one minute.'

To the sound of the tremendous cheer of hope that rose spontaneously all over the square, Matz fled for the door. There, as an afterthought, he paused, then ran back and grabbed the panties from beneath the unconscious officer's nose. 'Filthy perverted swine,' he chortled. 'Allus got yer conk in women's drawers. What is the officer corps coming to these days?' Then he was pelting down the stairs, with the roar of the storming soldiers growing louder by the second.

The platform was a scene of indescribable confusion, as the chaindogs turned to face the onslaught of the thousands of crazed field-greys who were determined to get on the train. Whistles blew shrilly. Red-faced angry officers bellowed orders. Chaindogs fired their pistols into the air, trying to stop the rush.

To no avail. The chaindogs were submerged by the soldiers. A confused mêlée broke out. Soldiers and MPs lay on the platform everywhere, pounding each other with their fists. An officer was sent flying through the window of the *abort*[1] and came to rest at the feet of a startled, pimply, young soldier squatting there, his pants around his ankles, a dirty French book in his free hand, taking solace in the only pleasure left to him. 'Can't one be shitting-well private *anywhere*?' he demanded indignantly.

Schulze hesitated no longer. 'All right, lads, here we go!' The young troopers needed no urging. They doubled forward from their hiding place, swung by Rosie, and clattered up the steps into the coach reserved for her girls. Schulze, in the lead, virtually threw the men inside. In a matter of seconds the train would move off.

Von Dodenburg sprang aboard, followed by Matz.

Rosie flashed Schulze a look. 'Well, come on Sergeant-Major, give a lady a leg up. And no trying to get yer big paw up my skirt, either.'

'Never, gracious madame. I am a cavalier of the old school.'

'Yer, I know. Yer take yer boots off when you do it.'

Schulze laughed happily. 'You are a lady after my own heart,' he chortled, and taking the strain of her enormous buttocks, he pushed her up, noting as he did so that she was minus her pants, and that he now knew why they called her Red-Rimmed Rosie. 'I think I'm gonna like you.'

With a clatter of steel wheels and the noisy hiss of escaping steam, the train began to roll forward. On all sides, fighting men broke off their brawls and ran towards it. But it was already too late. The train was gathering speed by the instant. The pale, anxious, angry faces became a blur, and then they were gone for good, and the furious yells and shrill whistles of the MPs died into nothingness. Schulze sat back in his wooden seat and grinned at his own sweating blackened face in the window, telling himself he had done it again.

[1] Lavatory.

SIX

'So there I was, ladies,' Matz was explaining, as he sat in the net looking down at the admiring whores, 'my tonsils as dry as dust, trying to get a drink o' milk out of the cow's teats. But the bitch just wouldn't stop still. Then she farted. Christ, was that a cloud of green smoke! Nearly blew me off my twinkle-toes. Of course, I knew then what the matter was. She had too much wind. So being the clever lad I was in those days, I lit a match and held it near her ass. It was a fatal thing to do, ladies, I can tell you that.'

'Why, Sergeant-Major Schulze?' asked one of the consumptive whores, who von Dodenburg thought wouldn't last out the month.

'The force of the gas stored up in her guts, that's why, my dear Fraulein,' Matz replied, flattered immensely by the sudden promotion. 'A flame came out – I bet you it was three metres in length! It really warmed up my nuts, I can tell you. Anyway, it set the old barn on fire, the farmer did his noddle, and I thought it was about time I volunteered my services – and that is how I came to be a member of SS Assault Regiment Wotan.'

Listening half-heartedly, well aware of Red-Rimmed Rosie's admiring gaze as she looked up at him like a well-nourished creamy cow, Schulze watched the lush French countryside roll by. He was at peace with the world. Half an hour before, Rosie had satisfied his inner pigdog with half a chicken, a loaf of French bread, a bottle of wine – and a very satisfactory bit of close combat in the coach toilet, with an irate general-staff officer rattling the locked door in vain, complaining that he had the shits and had to get in *immediately*, to which Schulze had responded by another vigorous shove of his muscular thighs, much to the delight of Red-Rimmed Rosie.

'Where you lot going, Rosie?' he asked lazily, forgetting Matz and his tall tales.

'Where the green moss, the Marie, the money is, of course,' the fat blonde madame replied, her dreamy look

126

replaced by one which read 'cash register – next customer, please.'

'And where's that, my little cheetah?' Schulze said, dreamily stroking one of her magnificent breasts.

'Where the stubble-hoppers are – the West Wall.[1] War or no war, they'll soon be wanting it again.'

'Yes, thank God for *it*,' Schulze breathed, squeezing her nipple half-heartedly. 'But the West Wall's a lot of bunkers and pillboxes and underground barracks. Don't seem very exciting to me, Rosie.'

'Perhaps, but it's very safe, Schulze. I've been bombed, shelled, fired on these last five years, in the course of – er – duty, trying to earn a few pennies for my old age, and I don't intend to go hop at this stage of the game. It seems to me that a nice deep underground bunker with a couple of kilometres of concrete above would make a good place to survive the war.'

'You might just be right there, Rosie,' Schulze agreed, watching the skinny whore lifting Matz's sexual apparatus, as if she were trying to judge its weight.

'Ten kilo,' Matz said cheekily from his perch on the luggage net. 'Or are yer checking to see if it's all there?'

'Just SOP,'[2] the girl said.

'What are you gonna do when you retire, Rosie?' Schulze asked.

'I've got my eye on a nice boarding house—'

'You did say *boarding* house, Rosie?'

'I did,' she said firmly, and went on, 'On the Rhine near Bad Honnef. I'd like to cater for old gentlemen—'

'I hope they've got thick fingers,' Schulze interrupted again, remembering the session in the locked lavatory.

'It won't be that kind of house at all. I'll cater for respectable elderly gentlemen, who are passed that kind of piggery. Gentlemen of good background with a nice pension, widowers and bachelors, who might think of their landlady in their wills.' She lowered her violet eyes de-

---

[1] German name for the Siegfried Line.
[2] Military jargon, meaning 'Standard Operating Procedure'.

murely and they disappeared momentarily in the forest of false eyelashes and mascaraed brows.

Schulze looked at her plump white face in admiration. 'You're a one, Rosie, you certainly are. If you want a partner for your – er – boarding house, I'm ready and willing any day. I'd even grease the stairs with soap to help the elderly gents on their way to a far better world up there.' He raised his eyes in mock piety to the dirty ceiling of the coach, decorated with the crude obscenities of five years of travelling soldiery.

But Sergeant-Major Schulze was not fated ever to grease the stairs of Red-Rimmed Rosie's planned boarding house, for Fate, with a capital F, had other plans in mind for him that day.

The tall American with the grizzled hair swigged from the metal canteen of martini cocktail which was always ready at his hip, and said to no one in particular, 'Why a chickenshit Kraut train?'

'Comment?' asked the tousled-haired French boy, crouched on the hill next to him. Like the rest of his 'irregulars', as the American liked to call them, he was clad in the uniform of a dead US recon. outfit he had found ambushed on the road east, the day after he had decided that being a war correspondent was too tame for him. Besides, the role of combat soldier, however irregular, would be good for sales in the post-war years. The American decided that one drink wasn't enough; he'd better have another, which he did, before making his decisions.

Squinting through his faded brown eyes, he estimated that the long train couldn't be making more than twenty miles an hour, and once it hit the steep gradient leading into Rambouillet, its speed would decrease even further. He made a quick calculation, and decided it would take the train half an hour yet to get to the town. It would be time enough.

Stretching himself to his full height, thrusting out his belly as he did so, he looked down at the skinny Frenchman. 'Okay, kid,' he said, in his fluent, if inaccurate, French, 'I want you to shin up the pole,' he indicated the telegraph pole, 'and get on the wire to Rambouillet.'

'Yessir, Papa,' the boy answered, his eyes full of admiration for this bold American in the nondescript uniform with the dimpled brown cheeks, pepper-and-salt beard, rolling gait and insatiable demand for drink in any and every form. 'And what do I say?'

'You say, kid, that the boys should get their fingers out of their chickenshit asses, and you should say that they should plant two mines – or some plastic – on the track as it runs round the bend into the station, and you should say that once they've hit the chickenshit train, they should rush it from the off-side of the track, not where the platform is. The Boche will instinctively head for the platform escape route. Okay, kid?' The American smoothed down the bang which hid his ever-increasing bald spot.

'Okay, Papa.'

'Then pop to, kid.'

While the Frenchman shinned rapidly up the telegraph pole, the big grizzled American decided he could do with another martini. This day he would 'bag' a train. Throughout his adult life he had been bagging animals all over the world, but this would be the first time he had gotten himself a train.

He smiled down at the canteen, his real solace these last years, pleased with himself. Ernest Hemingway had decided to take a hand in the affairs of what was left of SS Assault Regiment Wotan.

SEVEN

'What's that?' Matz asked. He had been to the lavatory, too, with one of the consumptive girls, but evidently her treatment had not been as thorough as that which Red-Rimmed Rosie had given Schulze for Matz was still wide awake, unlike the troopers snoring away the long slow hot August afternoon all around him.

'What's what?' Schulze said lazily.

'There's somebody out there,' Matz said, 'and if my eyes don't mistake me, the bastard's carrying a m.p. And he's wearing civvies.'

Schulze woke up completely. Thrusting his face close to the dirty window, he peered out. The long heavy train was chugging up a very long incline, puffing through a long fir-wooded chalk-sided valley which rose from the broad plain which stretched as far as the eye could see. But Schulze and Matz were not interested in the view. Their gaze was concentrated on the tiny figures crouched in the woods, observing the train's laboured progress towards Rambouillet.

Schulze looked anxiously at Matz. 'Are you thinking what I am?'

'Yes, Schulzi. The only armed civvies in this part of the country must belong to those slit-eared, cock-croppers of the Resistance.'

'Right.' Schulze grabbed his Schmeisser and leapt to his feet. 'Sir,' he said urgently, shaking his CO's shoulder.

With a start von Dodenburg woke up. 'What is it?' he demanded.

'Partisans, sir! We've just spotted half a dozen of the buggers in the woods yonder and they're certainly not picking mushrooms up there—'

The crash of the first mine exploding directly below the labouring locomotive merged almost instantly with the second. For a moment nothing seemed to happen. Then the locomotive rose from the tracks and came down again with a tremendous crash. Its boiler ruptured. Thick white steam poured from it. Behind it, the first hospital coach teetered on the buckled tracks. With a great rending of metal and splintering of heavy sleepers, it toppled over, spewing screaming nurses and wounded men, naked for the most part, onto the ground.

In an instant, all was wild confusion. Officers blew frantic whistles. Red-faced noncoms bellowed orders. Women screamed. Staff officers flung themselves to the floors of their coaches, wet with spilled champagne and cognac. Soldiers, dressing hastily and pulling on their helmets, were dropping to the concrete of the platform to be mowed down instantly by the well-sited machine-guns of the Resistance.

In their coach, one of the whores started to scream. Red-Rimmed Rosie doubled up her pudgy, beringed fist and punched her in the mouth. 'Knock it off, Lore!' she shouted, sending the whore tumbling back over the nearest seat, her skirts flying wildly to reveal that she wasn't a true blonde after all. 'They ain't got us yet.'

'Too true, they ain't,' Schulze snarled, his mind full of the new danger to that dream house on the Rhine. 'Sir, what's your orders?'

Von Dodenburg ducked hastily as a burst of machine-gun fire raked the coach, sending wood splinters flying everywhere and setting more of the whores off screaming. They knew what their fate would be if the Resistance caught them alive. Swiftly he sized up the situation. Their coach was the last of the whole train, and it had still not reached the top of the incline. 'All right, everybody to the rear of the coach. Come on, you men – and you women, too.'

Impressed by the urgency of the young colonel's order, men and women scrambled to the rear of the coach in wild confusion. He swung round on Schulze and Matz. 'You two, up front. Try to uncouple the link with the next coach. I'll get on to the roof and give you covering fire.'

The two noncoms waited no longer. Instinctively they understood what the CO was trying to do. They stamped through the confused mess of the coach. Von Dodenburg smashed the butt of his m.p. against the shattered glass. At the end of the coach, troopers were doing the same and were beginning to fire at the ambushers. Agilely, von Dodenburg swung himself through the window, ignoring the slugs which pattered off the sides of the train everywhere, and clambered onto the roof.

Down at the station there were partisans, everywhere, most in black sweat shirts with red scarves tied boldly around their necks. Red fire spat from the *pissoir*, the luggage hall, the waiting room. The ambush had been very carefully planned. The field-grey bodies sprawled on all sides on the bloody concrete were eloquent testimony to that. Von Dodenburg doubled across the sloping roof to the spot above which Schulze and Matz were hammering frantically at the coupling. He flung himself full length on the bakingly hot metal and started firing.

There was a hoarse cry of alarm from the partisans. They had guessed what the men in the last coach were attempting to do. More and more of them directed their fire on the two NCOs. Matz was stung a red-hot blow on his right cheek. He ran his hand up. Blood was pouring down his face. 'Horse-fly stung me,' he commented, and renewed his efforts to free the coupling with the butt of his m.p.

Abruptly the two sweat-drenched, frantic comrades had it. The coupling gave and the chain dropped with a clatter to the track. Von Dodenburg heard the sound above the snap and crackle of the small-arms fire. He dropped to the deck next to them. 'Back into the coach!' he yelled.

Already the last coach was beginning to move, slowly but surely. They doubled into the smoke-filled coach. 'One, two, three,' von Dodenburg yelled. 'Now jump together!'

Like a bunch of schoolgirls skipping in a schoolyard, the terrified whores did as he commanded, dresses and breasts flying. The coach started to move a little faster.

'You men, too!' von Dodenburg barked – urgently, well aware of the many feet running towards the coach to stop it before it could get away. '*Now!*'

Fifty pairs of dice-breakers crashed down in company with the women's lighter shoes. They did the trick. The coach started to roll down the gradient more swiftly, gathering speed by the instant, leaving behind a suddenly halted group of angry partisans. Now the countryside was hissing past, a crazy green blur. The coach rattled and trembled frighteningly. Most of the whores had flung themselves on the floor and were busy having hysterics there, in spite of the fact that Red-Rimmed Rosie was belabouring their ribs with well-directed kicks. Even the troopers were scared, and were hanging on to whatever they could find for all their worth.

The coach roared round a bend at a terrifying rate, its wheels screeching in protest at the strain. It was tearing down the incline at well over 100 kilometres an hour now. Von Dodenburg, clinging desperately to a stanchion, was beginning to congratulate himself that they had at least escaped the ambush, whatever else lay in store for them, when he saw it: the hastily erected barricade of oil-drums filled with concrete which the tiny figures below were shoving across the line. The bastards had thought of everything; they had cut the line behind them.

In exactly one minute they would hit the damned thing, and with the clarity of a sudden vision he knew exactly what would happen to them – SS troopers – once they fell into the bloody hands of the French Resistance. He sighed, and holding on tightly in anticipation of the great crash, he prepared to meet his fate at last . . .

EIGHT

'*On ne fait pas la guerre avec les femmes*', Hemingway said, as he sat on the steps of the *Hotel du Grand Veneur*, and sprayed the bluebottles which buzzed happily around the fresh corpse at his feet with a flitgun filled with eau de Cologne.

'But they are Boche, *mon Colonel*,' one of his sweating young irregulars protested. 'They are not women as we know them.'

Hemingway held out his hand without looking round, and the admiring waiter obligingly put a fresh glass of ice-cold Chablis into it. 'Shooting women is only for ballroom bananas and chickenshit canteen commandos,' the big writer persisted, and sipping his wine, he eyed the captured German women reflectively. The bedraggled whores were lined up in front of the sullen shabby SS men, who held their hands straight in the air, being prodded every now and again by the proud young partisans every time they looked as if they might lower them.

They looked awful. He doubted if he had ever seen worse-looking women, even in Cuba in the twenties. There was one of them with a dirty face, hair covered with a hood, who looked as if she could do with a good shave. He took another sip at the Chablis and said, 'Naturally you will shoot the men – they are SS. It is an obviousness. But for the women . . .' he gave one of the Gallic shrugs that he had been perfecting these last few crazy days since he had formed the 'irregulars'. 'I don't know. In Italy in '18, they didn't shoot the women, they raped them. That was a real war. In Spain in '36 they shot the women. That wasn't a real war. Now,' he finished the Chablis and held the glass out to the waiter, 'this, so they tell me, is a real war, so I conclude we must not shoot the women.'

There was a round of applause from the partisans at this judgment, but the young Frenchman was not satisfied. '*Mon Colonel*, undoubtedly you are very wise and have had great experiences in the wars. But those people you spoke of were not Boches. It is my suggestion that we shoot the men, then rape the prettier ones and shoot the ugly of them.'

Hemingway considered the suggestion for a while, enjoying the hot afternoon sun and listening to the hum of the bees in the honeysuckle at the back of the hotel, noting the sights and sounds, telling himself that he would not write this for *Collier's*,[1] but would save it for the big book on the war that he would write once he was back in Cuba.

'Perhaps you are right, kid,' he said lazily. 'But you will rape them on your own time, and in private. I'm not going to involve myself in trouble with the authorities for condoning rape. Shoot a couple of them you can, here and now. To encourage the others. Whom do you suggest?'

The partisan pointed to Red-Rimmed Rosie, who stood

[1] The magazine to which he was accredited as a war correspondent.

134

in the front rank glaring at them defiantly, one breast, the size of a sack of flour, exposed where the partisans had ripped her dress. 'That one – she kneed me in a private place,' he answered, somewhat aggrieved. 'That is bad for a man.'

'Always watch your *cojones*, kid,' Hemingway said cheerfully, finishing yet another glass of the ice-cold wine and telling himself that he would get this one down on paper right – every sight, every sound was printing itself on his mind. This time he'd write it the way it was. 'They're the things a boy should treasure most – after his mother, naturally,' he added hastily.

'Agreed, *mon Colonel*. And then that one—' he pointed to the huge woman who looked as if she badly needed a shave.

'Why her, kid?'

The partisan prodded the woman with his grease-gun and she advanced in an odd mincing step, her knees together under a skirt which looked as if it had been made hurriedly out of a tablecloth, with what looked like a pair of white flannel drawers peeping out at the hem.

'There's something wrong with her walk,' Hemingway said, and allowed his glass to be filled again.

The partisan ignored the remark. 'Because she looks so incredibly ugly,' he answered Hemingway's question. 'Nobody that ugly should be allowed to live. I shall be doing humanity a service if I kill her.'

He slammed his grease-gun into the woman's ribs and she shuffled forward in doomed despair, knees tight together, as she desperately attempted to prevent her drawers from falling.

Hemingway shuddered dramatically. 'God, she is ugly!' he exclaimed. 'Looks like Lon Chaney playing the hunchback of Notre Dame. Even I, chickenshit Hiawatha that I am, Ernie Hemorrhoid, the Poor Man's Pyle,[1] who has seen ugliness in all five continents, am shocked, deeply shocked. Yes, kid, I corrupt easily. Shoot the bitch!'

[1] A well-known war correspondent, killed in action in 1945.

The young partisan raised his grease-gun. Before he could fire, an ancient farmer began to lead a creaking old cart, filled high with steaming manure and pulled by a sway-backed mangy nag, between him and the women. He cursed angrily and lowered his m.p. It was a fateful thing to do.

Schulze let his skivvies drop. Ripping off the skirt made in that last panicky moment on the train from one of Red-Rimmed Rosie's treasured tablecloths, he pulled out the grenade he had hidden beneath it. With a tug he ripped off the china pin and flung it. In his haste he missed his selected target, the big drunken American. Instead the grenade landed right on top of the farmer's steaming manure.

A second later it exploded, showering the partisans with steaming horse apples, and assorted parts of the unfortunate nag.

Hemingway fell off his chair, swamped in manure, holding on to his glass with remarkable skill. The women started forward, scratching and tearing at the startled, manure-covered partisans. They reeled back under the sudden onslaught.

It was the chance that the SS men had been waiting for. Pausing only to cry, 'Well done, you big rogue!' at an uproariously laughing Schulze, von Dodenburg dived forward. His fist connected with the chin of the young partisan who had wanted to kill the women. He dropped like a stone. Von Dodenburg grabbed his grease-gun. Fortunately it was on 'fire'. Von Dodenburg pressed the trigger. Shooting from left to right, he sprayed the partisans with their own bullets, narrowly missing the big American, who was buried under the steaming horse apples. They went down on all sides.

The troopers of SS Assault Regiment Wotan were not slow to take advantage of the situation. Fighting their way through screaming women, who were punching and pulling the hair of the partisans still on their feet, they grabbed their weapons and began to run up the street and out of the town for the safety of the woods beyond.

Von Dodenburg yelled hastily, 'Spread out, and rendez-

vous in the woods! Every man for himself . . . Schulze and
Matz, take care of the women!'

'With pleasure!' Schulze bellowed, grabbing a machine-
pistol from a dying partisan.

'Watch it, yer knickers is showing,' Matz chortled, and
pointed a scornful dirty finger at Schulze's long johns. 'I
allus thought you were a bit twisted, Schulze.'

'I'll twist your turnip for you if you don't knock it off,'
Schulze snarled. 'Come on, let's get the women out of
danger!'

Next moment the whole pack of them, dirty unshaven
SS men and half-naked screaming harridans, were flying
for the safety of the woods.

Drunkenly, the big American clawed his way out of the
horse apples and looked moodily at the scene of death all
around him. Finally he took a sip at the Chablis and pro-
nounced his judgment. 'No dignity about it, no chickenshit
dignity at all.' Staggering to his feet, he barged through the
door of the *Hotel du Grand Veneur* in search of another
drink, leaving his 'irregulars' stiffening on the bloody, man-
ure-littered cobbles outside.

Thus it was that Wotan lived to fight another day, but
failed to enter the pages of the Great American War Novel.

NINE

'Ferk the army!' Matz toasted Schulze, raising the looted
demijohn of Calvados drunkenly to his lips, and letting a
small stream of it dribble down his unshaven chin as he
drank.

'Ferk France!' Schulze responded, raising his own demijohn in reply.

All around them, the women and those of the troopers
who drank were doing the same, indulging themselves in
the alcohol they had found in the huge cellars of the abandoned chateau HQ, trying to forget the shocks and alarms

137

of the last forty-eight hours. Von Dodenburg watched, sipping only a little from his own demijohn, knowing that they deserved this time out of war. He had sentries posted up above and they had placed *Achtung, Minen* notices on every approach road and lane. So he felt they were reasonably safe, even if they were drunk as lords for the most part.

'Ferk Germany too!' Matz was saying.

'Ferk the *whole* continent!' Schulze cried.

'Ferk the *whole* world!' Matz responded, and nearly missed his mouth with his demijohn, sending a great stream from it over the lap of a young trooper who had found some lemonade powder and was busy mixing it with water.

'Hey, knock it off!' the trooper cried indignantly.

Matz stared at the soaking wet patch around the indignant boys' flies. 'That's what comes of drinking water,' he said thickly, swaying dangerously, 'pisses yersen – and that reminds me, did you know that fishes ferk in water?'

Von Dodenburg smiled indulgently and forgot the antics of his two veterans.

They had been marching east for forty-eight hours now, and still they had not reached a stable German line. Twice they had thought they had arrived at a firm front, only to be told shamefacedly by the officer-in-charge that he and his men were 'moving on'. A whole army was on the run, with Patton's tanks at their heels, and nothing seemed able to make them turn and fight.

Von Dodenburg had lost his map-case days before, and now he racked his brain in an attempt to remember the terrain. The Amis had already crossed the Seine. That was out. For all he knew, Paris was probably already taken. He forced his mind to remember the geography of Northern France. But there seemed no physical feature where the army might turn and fight.

The Meuse. That was a possibility. Perhaps on the River Meuse, the German High Command might make a stand. The river was broad, and on the eastern bank there were high bluffs. If defence preparations had been made, it would be a tough nut for the enemy to crack. Von Dodenburg did a quick calculation and estimated that in their present weary condition, and marching cross-country, what was left of Wotan might make the river in another forty-eight hours.

He shook his head wearily, the drunken chatter all around him completely forgotten. That would be too late. The enemy, cutting easily through the defeated German army with their armour, would be on the western bank of the Meuse long before then; and Wotan didn't stand a chance of breaking through the enemy line.

He took a sip of his drink. Matz and Schulze, arms round each other's shoulders, and supported by Red-Rimmed Rosie, who for some reason had removed her skirt to reveal thighs like fleshy girders, were singing the exploits of that well-known grenadier and his sexual exploits with pigs, ending each scurrilous verse with the refrain '*jig-jig, fat little pig.*'

'So he put the juicy little pigs on wheels,' Schulze was bawling at the top of his voice.

Von Dodenburg sat up suddenly, his tiredness forgotten. *Wheels!* Of course, that's what they wanted – wheels. But where were they going to find the four or five vehicles needed to transport his troopers and the whores? What was left of the German army was on foot. They had abandoned what few vehicles they had left, either because of lack of fuel or from fear of the enemy *Jabos*. No, military vehicles were out of the question, even if they could be found.

For a moment or two, he toyed with the idea of perhaps attacking a lonely farm and looting some form of transport there. But he soon dismissed the idea. The local farms, what he had seen of them, seemed too poor for the farmers to have more than a cart, or a couple of oxen to draw it. There would be no motor vehicles to be found there.

In the bigger places, there would be cars and trucks, he knew. But there was no petrol for civilians, and civilians were forced to use wood-burning cars, the *gazogènes*. They would be far too slow for Wotan's needs. Suddenly he had it. In an instant he had the whole idea worked out in all its daring simplicity.

'Listen!' he said urgently, springing to his feet.

The drunken singing and chatter continued. Lent new energy and vitality by the strength of his idea, he grabbed his demijohn and smashed it violently against the stone wall, sloshing spirits everywhere.

The gesture worked. Startled men and women turned to stare at the tall young officer, his weary, dirty, unshaven features animated by sudden resolve. 'I want you all – women and men – to listen to me. It's vitally important.'

Schulze's comment died on his lips. He knew the CO. He wiped the back of his hand across his wet mouth and listened.

'I don't have to tell you what a fix we are in,' von Dodenburg said, staring round at their faces, almost hidden in the gloom. 'To be completely honest with you, the German army in the west is *kaputt*. It hasn't a chance. According to my calculations therefore, the only chance we have of not being slaughtered by the partisans or ending up in some Ami cage is to get over onto the eastern bank of the River Meuse before the enemy reaches the river. I'm sure we'll stand a chance then. But we're going to need vehicles to do that – and vehicles which will rouse the mistrust of neither the enemy, or the gentlemen of the White Army.'[1]

There was a mutter of agreement from the men, somewhat sobered up now by the urgency of their CO's words. They had all heard of the soldiers' tales of what had happened to German soldiers who had been unlucky enough to fall into the hands of the White Army. 'Yer can end up as a singing tenor with those bastards – right smartish,' Schulze ventured, making a quick cutting gesture low down on his body for the benefit of the puzzled whores.

'Even without one, *you'd* still be at it,' Red-Rimmed Rosie, angered by Schulze's recent attempts to wander off with

[1] The Belgian Resistance.

140

other whores, commented sourly. 'But what do you suggest, sir?' she addressed herself to von Dodenburg.

'This. The only vehicles in Northern France which arouse no suspicion this August are those of the enemy.'

'So?'

Von Dodenburg grinned at her bewildered face. 'So, my dear lady, I think it is time that Wotan possessed itself of American wheels.'

Von Dodenburg raised his hands to stop the excited chatter, and waited for the first question.

It came quickly, and from Schulze. *'When?'* he snapped, seemingly completely sober now. *'Where* and *how?'*

'Now,' von Dodenburg barked back with equal energy, 'on the main Amiens-Reims highway.'

There were gasps of surprise from the men. All of them knew that the main highways were completely under enemy control, with their fighter-bombers patrolling them during the daylight hours, ready to knock out the slightest German resistance.

'As for the *how*, I'll tell you about that later. Now then, the lot of you, get rid of those damned bottles and ready yourself!' Von Dodenburg raised his voice above the sudden noise as the troopers struggled to their feet and started searching the straw, which covered the stone floor, for their equipment. 'Madame Rosie, I wonder if I could have a few words with you?' he called.

Delicately holding her hands above the dark smudge at the base of her considerable stomach, as if she were some simpering teenage virgin, Red-Rimmed Rosie, flattered by the handsome aristocratic officer's attention, came towards him. Seconds later the two of them were deep in conversation, while the men of Wotan prepared for their last operation of the war on French soil.

TEN

'Sheet!' the coloured corporal hissed though suddenly clenched teeth. '*Poon Tang!*' He hit the brakes. Next to him, his dozing assistant woke up with a start, wondering why the big deuce-and-a-half truck was no longer moving.

'Whatya say, Washington?' he said thickly, sitting upright on the hard cab seat.

'Just get a load of *that*!' his companion sighed and stared through the gloom at the sudden appearance which had made him brake so hard.

Benny, his companion, followed the direction of his transfixed gaze.

Outlined by the faint light given off by the blacked-out headlights, he, too, saw the woman. She was fat, but white, clothed solely in a black silk slip which ended at her plump waist and a pair of black net stockings rolled up at the knee. And she was sitting there on the kilometre marker, as if it was the most obvious thing in the world to be there in the middle of the night, half-naked. Benny gave a faint whistle and said, 'What now, Brother Washington?'

Brother Washington, well-known for his amorous progress from Chicago to Chester, didn't even look round. 'Are you kidding, Benny?'

He let out the clutch, and in first gear began to crawl up the road to the spot where the fat white woman was waiting. With a hasty gesture of his black muscular arm, he pulled the brake. 'Hey sister, you want ride? . . . *Promenez* with the *camion*?' He beamed down at her, all gleaming white teeth and sick yellow eyes, noting with interest that she shaved her pubic hair, always a good sign for bed, he told himself.

When the woman didn't move, but kept on staring up at him in silence, he jerked his thumb towards the back of the truck. 'We got *café* and *cigarettes*. You jig-jig with Washington Lee Jeffers and his buddy Benny and you're in the chips, baby. *Café* and *cigarettes*,' he repeated the words carefully and loudly so that his generous offer was quite clear to her. 'For jig-jig.'

'*Oui*,' the woman said and straightened up.

Washington flashed a big-toothed look at Benny. 'Okay, Benny, you take a little walk. Me and the lady are gonna do a little jiving in the cab.'

Benny looked a little worried. 'It's goddam dark out there, Washington,' he protested, 'and the Captain said there might still be Krauts about on the back roads.'

'Beat it, buddy! That whitey Captain'd shit his britches at the sight of a iddy-biddy mouse. Haul ass, friend,' he added, tugging at his belt, 'Washington Lee Jeffers is gonna get himself some o' that white tail in a goddam hurry!'

Mumbling to himself, Benny dropped out of the cab as the woman walked round to meet his companion. But he didn't get far. Just as he crossed the ditch at the side of the road, looking for a spot where he could sit down and wait his turn, and eyeing the silent French countryside a little anxiously, a big hand reached out from behind a tree. He was lifted from his feet, his cry of alarm strangled at birth. While he dangled there helplessly, another hand reached out and removed his helmet. Next moment a heavy club came down on the back of his crew-cut skull and Benny knew no more for a while.

When Benny came to again, he found he was minus his uniform. Now he was clad only in his olive-drab underwear. 'What happened?' he moaned and stared around at the hard bearded faces that were staring down at him in the faint light cast by the headlights of the truck. Then he saw the silver SS runes, and his dark eyes rolled around in absolute panic. 'Jesus – the SS!'

'*Schnauze!*'[1] snapped the little wizened soldier, with a wooden leg, who was pulling on his uniform.

Benny turned his aching head with a groan. Washington, nursing a swollen cheek, was standing outside the cab, sullenly watching the fat white woman putting on her skirt,

[1] 'Hold your trap'.

while a young, desperate-looking SS man held his rifle pointed at Washington's ribs. 'Washington,' he called piteously, 'what they gonna do to us?'

'*Schnauze*!' Matz snapped again, and rammed his wooden leg into Benny's side routinely and without malice. 'All right, sir, I'm finished.'

'Good,' von Dodenburg answered from the back of the truck, where he had supervised his men while they hid their weapons behind the crates. He turned to Red-Rimmed Rosie. 'You did an excellent job, Madame Rosie. I'm grateful to you. Now take those cigarettes and get back inside the chateau. My men will ensure that you're all right – and you can rest assured we'll be back to fetch you all once we've got the other trucks.'

'A pleasure – a pleasure, Colonel,' Red-Rimmed Rosie said grandly. Accepting the three looted cartons of Camels from von Dodenburg, she began to walk back to the chateau where the rest, who were not going on the operation, were waiting. Then, with an afterthought, she stopped and raised her skirt so that a sullen Washington got a swift glimpse of her enormous behind. 'There you are, sonny – something to remember me by.' Laughing uproariously, she disappeared into the darkness, followed by two grinning young troopers, who were eating looted chocolate and herding a shaking Benny in front of them.

A minute later, the truckload of 'Kraut POWs' was on its way, with a sullen, bleeding, Washington at the wheel, a blackened-face Matz crouched next to him, a pistol dug deep into the big Negro's ribs. Stage Two of the operation was underway.

They crept carefully up the narrow winding street, paved with ancient cobbles, towards the sound of the accordion, their eyes fixed on the trucks, which meant escape. Behind them the rest of the 'POWs' were grouped around a glowering Washington, weapons concealed under their camouflaged tunics. The evening air was full of tension.

Wordlessly, von Dodenburg nodded to Matz. Boldly, he

stepped to the first truck and pulled open the door. Chewing gum and hoping that if any French civvie saw him, he would be taken for an *ami*, he pressed the starter. Nothing happened! He did so again. Nothing save a low weak groan. Matz cursed and went to the next truck, grateful that the music coming from inside the blacked-out *bistro* covered any noise he might make. Swiftly he clambered in the cab and turned the attached key. Once more the engine didn't start. Cursing fluently, he tried again – with the same result. Dropping to the ground, he flung back the hood and saw immediately what the trouble was. In spite of their hurry to get inside the *bistro* to the girls and the drink, the Ami drivers had still carefully immobilized their trucks. They had taken the distributor caps with them.

A moment later he had explained the situation to von Dodenburg. For a second the CO was silent, his face creased in a thoughtful frown. Then he made his decision. 'All right, listen. We're going to have to risk it. Sooner or later our luck is going to run out and we'll be spotted.'

The little group of men around him nodded their agreement.

'We've got to have those distributor caps – and the only place we're going to get them is inside that pub. Schulze?'

'Sir?'

'Get round the back. See if you can get inside. If there's trouble you can bale us out.'

'I'll try to find the piss corner, sir. I'll work my way in from there.' Remarkably silent for such a big man, he doubled away, m.p. clutched like a toy in his ham of a fist.

Von Dodenburg turned to Matz. 'Do you speak English, Matz?'

Matz grinned up at him. 'It's a long way to Tipperary,' he said with an atrocious accent, 'God shave the King.'

Von Dodenburg stroked his yellow-bearded chin. 'Afraid we're not going to get very far with your knowledge of the language, Matz. All right, this is what we'll do. I'm going in there as your prisoner. Your uniform should get us there

145

without trouble. After that, I'll take over. The rest of you cover the door. If any civilians come along, deal with them.'

Matz grinned at his worried CO. 'Think nothing of it, sir. Old Matzi'll see you through.'

Von Dodenburg's only reaction was a doubting sniff, and the comment, 'All right, linguist, in you go.'

Aware that his hand was trembling slightly, von Dodenburg pushed aside the thick felt blackout curtain which covered the door and entered, followed by Matz, holding his American grease-gun levelled at his CO's back.

The smoke and noise slapped von Dodenburg almost physically in the face. The long narrow *bistro* was divided up into small wooden alcoves, crowded with drunken sweating GIs, drinking their wine straight from the bottle, and sluttish, flushed women who sat on the Negroes' knees, powdered arms clasped round their necks as if they had known them for years and not for only minutes. To the rear, on the raised platform used for *Le Dancing*, three ancient Frenchmen with cigarettes glued to their bottom lips and dark berets perched on the backs of their heads were belting out *bal musette* music, with much pounding of the big drum and clashing of the cymbals, to a completely unreceptive audience. At the zinc bar, run by a big white-blonde, its surface awash with spilled wine, happy Negro soldiers laughed and joked with fat whores; and the smoke-blue air was full of their unrestrained laughter and the giggles of the drunken women.

Von Dodenburg looked around swiftly, as he stood there at the door with Matz poised behind him, the two of them as yet unnoticed by the Amis. There were about twenty Negroes in the *bistro* and they all carried big .45 pistols at their hips, tied down to their thighs by a leather thong so that they looked like the cowboys he remembered from his youthful film-going, only these cowboys were black. 'Matz,' he whispered from the side of his mouth, 'I take the bar – you the alcove. Clear?'

'Clear.'

'Right, in we go.'

146

Their every nerve jingling with tension, the two of them advanced into the smoke-filled, noisy room, the palms of their hands sweating at the knowledge of what was to come.

Now the soldiers became aware of their presence. 'What you bringing that guy in here for, buddy?' a Negro demanded.

'*Un boche!*' a whore gasped.

Purposefully the two strangers advanced into the centre of the room.

'Don't you speak American, brother?' the voice was cool, clear and incisive, unlike the unintelligible drawl of the other Negroes. Colonel von Dodenburg turned his head to look at the speaker. Nature had played a cruel trick on the Negro who had spoken. His features were perfect – straight chiselled nose, fine strong jaw, lofty brow, framed by close-cropped black hair – and he carried himself with natural authority. The man, von Dodenburg couldn't help thinking, would have been perfect for a recruiting poster, but for one thing. He was black.

Von Dodenburg stopped, working his fingers towards the pistol he carried in his pocket, staring anxiously at the handsome black man; he knew trouble when he saw it.

'You got hearing trouble, soldier, or something?' the handsome Negro said, addressing himself to a puzzled Matz. 'Bad enough a whitey like you coming in here to spoil our fun, but then you bring a Kraut with you. Well, whatya say?'

'You tell him, Sarge,' the other Negroes urged happily, pleased to see this confrontation between their top kick and the white man in a segregated army where the lowest white Pfc had more say than the most senior black noncom. 'Zap it to him!'

'Knock it off,' Master-Sergeant Lee said out of the side of his mouth, his eyes suddenly suspicious. 'I asked you a question, whitey, what do you say?' Slowly but surely, his big black hand started to slide down to the pistol at his side.

Von Dodenburg hesitated no longer. He flashed his own

pistol out. 'Hands up!' he commanded. 'Back up against the bar.'

The fat whores screamed. Negroes cursed. Next to von Dodenburg, Matz swung his grease-gun threateningly in the direction of the men and women in the alcoves. 'Get yer flippers up!' he snarled. The Negroes might not have understood his German, but they understood the gesture well enough. Their black hands shot into the air.

'All right,' von Dodenburg said, selecting his words with care, 'I want all drivers to come forward – one by one – and put the—' he couldn't think of the English word for distributor cap and said, 'the thing they took from their motor on the bar. Right, now – the first one.'

A badly frightened runty Negro slipped from under the fat frizzy-haired French woman who sat on his lap, and came forward hesitantly. He put the precious distributor cap on the wet zinc surface of the bar.

'Thank you,' von Dodenburg said politely. 'Now the next one.'

Another Negro, fat and bull-like, rose uncertainly to his feet, embarrassed because the whore who sat next to him had undone his flies. With his underpants showing, he advanced to the bar, trying to button up his trousers with his free hand. Unconsciously attracted by the Negro's embarrassed attempts to cover himself, von Dodenburg took his eyes off the bar for a moment. The handsome Negro seized his opportunity. He thrust his foot out. The fat one stumbled and fell against von Dodenburg, sending him staggering against one of the whores. She screamed and dropped off the bar stool. The next instant the Negro Sergeant had jerked out his pistol and fired, the slug hissing by Matz's skull, missing him by a hair's breadth.

In a flash all was chaos. A bullet shattered the light. Red hot glass showered down on von Dodenburg. Momentarily blinded he attempted to grab the two precious distributor caps. The handsome Negro fired again. The scarlet flame stabbed the confused blackness. Desperately von Dodenburg fumbled along the wet counter. At his feet the crouched whores were screaming hysterically. Then he had them. 'Matz,' he yelled above the racket. 'Back off. I've got them.'

'With you, sir.'

'Me, too!' It was Schulze. Crashing through the back door, he fired a wild burst at the ceiling. Plaster came raining down like snow. With one fist cradling the sub-machine gun under his arm, he grabbed a bottle of spirits as he blundered by the bar. A woman stumbled into him. 'Christ, missus,' he gasped, 'a bloke has to be protected against sharp tits like that! Could stab a feller to death!' Laughing uproariously, he flung open the felt curtain and ran into the evening gloom.

'Come on, you yeller bastards!' Master-Sergeant Lee yelled angrily when no one moved. '*Nigger yeller bastards!*'

The insult had its effect. Grabbing for their weapons, the surprised soldiers headed for the door, blundering and stumbling into the hysterical whores in the confused darkness. Lee thrust aside the curtain and dived with all his strength towards the horse-watering trough next to the entrance.

A vicious burst of fire stitched a trail of blue sparks on the cobbles just behind him. Crouching behind the stone trough, he took careful aim. A German fanned the air with his hands wildly. His knees gave beneath him weakly and he sank to the ground.

'Stop the black bastards!' a German cried.

A salvo of m.p. fire cut the air. The Negroes running out of the door went down screaming in a confused wild mess of arms and legs – and blood. Lee cursed. 'Through the windows, you dumb bastards!' he ordered, and fired again. Another German grunted thickly and went down, clutching his suddenly useless knee.

Lee waited. Behind him he could hear the rest smashing windows. When they were out, he'd order them to come in from left and right and try to outflank the Krauts. Grimly his eyes flashed to the trucks. There the Kraut dressed in GI uniform was flinging back the hood of one of the trucks. To put in the distributor cap, Lee realized at once. He aimed and fired. He missed. He could hear the slug howl away from the metal. '*Shit!*' he cursed and fired again.

The slug hit the hood and the little Kraut dropped. Lee could see he wasn't hit. But the bullets were keeping him from getting the distributor fixed. Without that the Krauts couldn't get away. Schulze realized that too. He didn't hesitate. They were virtually trapped. From further inside the town, he could hear the wail of sirens and the roar of many wheels. The fire-fight had alerted the local garrison. If they didn't get on their way in a minute, they'd be finished. 'Apeturd, get ready with that distributor – *I'm going in!*'

Dropping his gun to the cobbles, he hurtled forward. Lee saw him coming. He fired. The slug howled off the cobbles just to the Kraut's front. He fired again. Once more he missed. Then the big enraged Kraut was on him. Lee dropped his empty pistol and grabbed for the German's throat.

His big black hands connected. Schulze gasped and threw his head back. His helmet rolled to the ground. But still Lee did not relax his grasp. Instead he exerted more and more pressure, throwing his big muscular body backwards a little so that he could utilize his full strength. Desperately Schulze flashed up his knee. The black avoided it easily. His hands were now cutting deep into Schulze's throat. Schulze's ears were full of a great roar. Red violent, electric lights were beginning to flash before his eyes. Almost overcome by panic, he knew he would black out in a moment if he didn't break that hold.

Twisting with all his strength, he forced the Negro onto his side. Still Lee held on, the sweat streaming down his black face in great rivulets. Gasping fearfully, Schulze thrust his heavy thigh against Lee's. The Negro tried to avoid it. Schulze persisted. With the last of his strength, feeling he was going to black out now, he heaved.

Lee flew through the air, to come crashing down heavily onto the cobbles. Gulping in great gasps of blessed air, Schulze, bleeding from his nose and ears, staggered forward. '*Brave . . . black . . . bastard*,' he gasped and brought down his cruel, nailed, heavy boot right into the centre of Lee's upturned face. He screamed and went limp.

The next instant there was the throaty wild roar of the first truck starting up. The second followed a fraction of a second later. Stick grenades hissed through the air. They caught the first group of Negroes attempting to clamber out of the shattered side window. They flew backwards into the *bistro*. No more attempted to follow.

In wild, panicky confusion, the Wotan men clambered into the roaring trucks, aware that the wail of the sirens were getting ever louder. Matz and von Dodenburg slammed home first gear. As the first carload of MPs shot round the corner, firing as they came, the truck, driven by Wotan's CO, vanished into the night.

ELEVEN

The long procession of gleaming scout cars and half-tracks, bristling with machine guns held by immaculate MPs, their tall antennas whipping crazily overhead, came hurtling down the street. Frantically the French civilians scattered for cover into the nearest doorways, eyes popping at the sight of the officer standing upright in the lead scout car, its siren shrieking hideously.

General George Patton stood in the front of the scout car like a charioteer, wearing his 'war face', his jaw jutting against the webbing strap of his lacquered helmet with its outsize triple stars. The situation in the French town was untidy and 'Blood-an'-Guts' Patton hated untidy situations. 'Okay, driver,' he commanded in that high-pitched voice of his. 'This is where the dusky warriors fought their last battle.' He pointed his crop at the bodies sprawled next to the bullet-riddled trucks.

The driver halted, as did the rest of the convoy. Patton sprang out. Behind him MPs did the same, taking up their defensive positions, their grease-guns directed at the awed

French civilians as if they expected them to attempt to rush the general at any moment.

Imperiously, the army commander strode across the cobbles, kicking away the litter as he went, to where the dead Negroes lay sprawled in the extravagant attitudes of the violently done to death. His faded blue eyes blazed with sudden anger. 'Goddammit,' he snarled, 'Goddammit to hell!'

He ben next to a grey-haired aidman who was kneeling over an unconscious Negro, pencilling the morphine dosage he had just given the wounded soldier on his forehead with a red crayon. 'What happened, soldier?' he asked, his voice gentler.

The aidman, his back to the commanding general and engrossed in his task, grunted, 'Bushwhacked. Some Krauts got them when they was in the bar.'

'And the Krauts?'

'Search me, buddy,' the aidman began, then something told him he was in the presence of authority. He turned and looked up from his task, to be confronted by Patton's craggy face under the gleaming helmet. 'Christ on a crutch!' he breathed, '*Old Blood-an'-Guts* – sorry, sir,' he corrected himself immediately. 'There's one of them dead Krauts over there – next to the horse trough.'

'Carry on, soldier, you're doing a fine job,' Patton said automatically, using one of the set phrases he always had ready for his men when he was pleased with them. 'Fine job.'

Briskly he strode across to the dead man, clad in the camouflaged smock of the Armed SS. His nose wrinkled in disgust, he turned the body over with the toe of his gleaming riding boot.

A boyish face with hardly a trace of beard stared up at him, the eyes blank and vacant. 'SS,' the General said. 'Codman,' he turned to his aide, 'find out his outfit.'

Codman sniffed but said nothing. Delicately, hating what he had to do, trying not to breathe in the stench of death,

Colonel Codman rolled up the sleeve to reveal the black and silver armband of the SS beneath.

'The goddam Wotan!' Patton exploded when he saw. 'SS Assault Regiment Wotan! I thought the goddam Limeys had finished them off at Falaise. Now the sons of bitches are swanning around in my territory, doing exactly what they goddam like.' Swiftly Patton worked himself up into one of his artificial rages, while Codman stood patiently at the general's side. He knew the Old Man. The rages were meant more for the benefit of the onlookers than anything else: it was a tried and trusted method Patton often used to get things done, when faced by reluctant or scared subordinates. At heart the Old Man was a sentimental softie, who wept often and copiously. Studying his boots thoughtfully, and not really listening, he waited till the usual tirade was over, wondering idly what the French must think of them, the Americans.

'Dingy warriors or not,' Patton concluded, his face flushed angrily, 'they are American soldiers and they must not die in vain. Codman, get me Wood on the phone.'

Five minutes later Patton was giving his orders to General Wood, the commander of his favourite outfit, the 4th Armoured Division, ending with the ominous words, 'Wood, I want you guys to pick up your marbles and wipe out these Wotan bastards. Otherwise I'll have to start thinking about a change in command. *Heads might roll . . .*'

Colonel Creighton Abrams, Commander of the 37th Tank Battalion, took the unlit stump of his cigar out of his mouth, and looked around at his battalion officers. 'Gentlemen,' he announced, 'as usual the buck has stopped at the old 37th. The General passed it on to his Deputy. The Deputy passed the buck to the Combat Command Leader who obligingly passed it on to me.' He grinned at them. 'The shit has hit the fan and we're the poor suckers who've got to pick it up again.'

'What happened, sir?' one of the officers asked.

'Old Blood-an'-Guts has handed us another beaut.'

'Yeh, that's nothing new. You know what they call him in the Fourth – his guts, our blood,' someone commented.

'Roger,' Abrams agreed, and then his grin vanished. 'OK, gentlemen, this is the big picture. Some of those SS bastards from the Wotan outfit hijacked one of our convoys and took off in their trucks. Now all the Old Man wants us to do is to find the SS and eliminate them. As easy as that.' His paunch shivered as he gave a cynical, throaty laugh. *'Generals!'*

'Well, we know they're heading east,' someone ventured.

'Sure,' Abrams agreed, 'as are some one hundred thousand other Krauts. Big deal.'

'Agreed,' the man who had spoken said, 'But if we started where they hijacked our convoy we might be able to figure out their general direction.'

Abrams nodded his approval. 'Yeah, that's true. They bushwhacked the convoy at the outskirts of Amiens.' He turned and stabbed his cigar against the map hanging from the side of his command Sherman. 'Here. And we know that they're heading for the general line of Verdun–Liège on the Meuse – here and here.'

'That's one helluva lot of country, Colonel,' ventured Second-Lieutenant van Horn, the Third, the newest replacement officer in the 37th.

Abrams paused and stared at the handsome young officer, whom he knew belonged to one of Boston's oldest families, as if he were seeing him for the very first time. 'That is a very telling remark, van Horn,' he said, the sarcasm undisguised in his gravelly voice, 'but what would you suggest?'

Van Horn flushed suddenly, realizing that he had said too much. 'Well, sir,' he began hesitantly, 'I took a year of military history at Harvard—' There was sudden laughter from the West Pointers among the 37th's officers, but van Horn did not let himself be stopped, '– and we did the frontier fortresses during the course – Verdun, Metz and the like.'

'And pray where is this leading us, van Horn, the serious

154

student of military history?' Abrams said, his chubby face wreathed in a grin.

'Well, sir, I think we can eliminate certain spots on the Meuse where the Germans won't hold. Consequently these SS guys won't be heading for those spots.'

'For instance?'

'Well, sir, they won't hold Verdun. They've got Metz as a better fortification. The Maginot Line and all that. So if they don't hold Verdun, they'll allow the whole of the French Meuse Line to go. So my guess is,' van Horn hurried on, growing confidence in his voice, 'that they'll hold the line of the Belgian Meuse – say between Huy or Dinant and Liège. The terrain there is pretty rugged. At Harvard, our Prof—'

Abrams held up his hand. 'Spare me the pearls of military wisdom your Prof cast before the Harvard swine,' he said urgently, his chubby face suddenly thoughtful, as he stared at the map. 'Between Huy – here in the south, and Liège – here in the north.' He chewed on his cigar. 'Brother, that's still a lot of ground to cover.'

'Yeah,' the second-in-command agreed, 'and there's thousands of goddam deuce-and-a-half trucks around.'

'But not that many in the retreating German army,' van Horn butted in with youthful enthusiasm. 'If we could get the spotter plane up, it could report any two-and-a-half ton trucks seen among the enemy forces, sir.'

Abrams turned on him. 'You know, van Horn, you're beginning to grow on me. You're not all pretty face.'

Van Horn beamed.

'Okay, gentlemen, this is the way we're gonna do it. I'll break the battalion into companies. Each company will have a different route, but each will work its way east towards the River Meuse, keeping in radio contact with the spotter. Once it gives us the good word, we concentrate, in the hope that the pilot has found the right Krauts. 'Kay?'

There was a murmur of agreement from the assembled officers.

'And remember this, gentlemen, we've got to find those

goddam Krauts,' he paused significantly, remembering the exact words which had come down from the 'head shed',[1] or 'heads are gonna roll'.

Colonel Abrams tossed away his cigar. 'All right, gentlemen, don't stand around like spare dildoes in a convent. Let's get on the stick. Roll 'em!'

The officers saluted, and turning, began to double back to the waiting Shermans, where the drivers were already starting to gun their engines, filling the still afternoon with noise and thick blue smoke.

'Van Horn.'

The young Lieutenant with the innocent face stopped in mid-stride. 'Sir?'

'That was a pretty fine piece of thinking you just did.'

Van Horn flushed with pleasure.

'And because of it, I'm going to give you the honour of taking the point.'

'Thank you, sir,' van Horn gushed. 'I certainly do appreciate it.'

'Okay, son, on your way,' Abrams said and pulled out another cigar.

Hastily, his face revealing his happiness at the honour, van Horn saluted and ran to his waiting Sherman *Harvard Crimson*.

'Sucker,' Abrams told himself, watching him go, eager, or so it appeared, to die quickly. 'There's one born every minute.' Then he, too, hauled his bulk on board the command Sherman and got on with the bloody business of war.

TWELVE

'The thin crust, Lootenant,' Big Red Anderson, van Horn's sergeant, whispered.

Van Horn stared down the moonlit road. Up ahead there was the pink glow of artillery, silhouetting the stark black

[1] GI slang for Headquarters.

outlines of his waiting armoured cars and Shermans. Somewhere a kraut machine-gun chattered hysterically and white
tracer zipped through the night. But so far the men in the
village ahead did not suspect the Americans had caught up
with them yet again.

'Once we're through that particular bunch of Heinies,'
the huge red-haired veteran of the last month's fighting
said, 'there's nothing to stop us until we reach the river,
Lootenant.'

Van Horn nodded his agreement, studying the situation.
There was no time for any fancy tactical planning. It would
have to be straight down the highway and right through
them, hoping that boldness, dash and surprise would scat-
ter the enemy before they had time to react. Abrams had
been riding him all day by radio to push on, and he didn't
want another chewing-out from the plump West Pointer.

He pressed the throat mike and gave his order. 'Okay,
driver, roll 'em!'

With a roar, *Harvard Crimson*'s motors burst into life.
The Sherman lumbered onto the road, and suddenly the
night was hideous with the clatter of tracks and the racket
of tank motors. At fifty kilometres an hour, the armoured
column hit the village.

Abruptly the village woke. Shouts, screams, orders,
counter-orders came from all sides. A sentry in a ditch fired
his *panzerfaust*.[1] The rocket zipped through the darkness,
trailing fiery-red sparks behind it. An armoured car staggered to a stop, slewing round in a violent skid as its front
tyres burst under the impact. White smoke started to pour
from its engine. Someone fired a burst of m.g. fire. The
bazooka-man's face disappeared in bloody gore.

'Look out, Lootenant!' Big Red yelled in alarm.

Van Horn ducked instinctively. A slug howled off the
turret, inches away. He pressed the trigger of his .45, feeling somehow like a cowboy in some Hollywood shoot-up.
From an upper window, the German, who had fired at him,

[1] German bazooka.

screamed and smashed to the cobbles. Next moment *Harvard Crimson*'s flailing tracks tore him to pieces.

Now the Shermans began to roll back and forth up the village street, spraying the upper windows of the houses on both sides with machine-gun fire. Germans started to slam to the cobbles everywhere. Grinning hugely, obviously enjoying every moment of it, Big Red pulled the pin out of a phosphorus grenade and slung it through a shattered upper window. In a flash the building was ablaze. Screaming hideously, German soldiers, their uniforms burning furiously, came running into the street, their faces contorted with absolute horror. The 37th men didn't hesitate. Fourteen .50 calibre machine-guns concentrated on them, the lead whipping them back and forth like powerless puppets in the hands of a suddenly crazy puppeteer, until they finally dropped to the bloody cobbles, lifeless, their flesh already beginning to blacken in the intense, all consuming heat.

Van Horn's nostrils were assailed by the stench of charred human flesh. He felt nauseated, sensing the bile beginning to rise in his throat. He fought the feeling. He knew he must not indulge in pity. The burning men were the enemy.

Up ahead, a new danger presented itself. A group of Germans in their underwear were fumbling frantically with a 88mm. cannon. Obviously they were trying to bring it to bear on the column. 'Gunner—'

'Knock that sonuvabitch out!' Big Red beat him to it. The Sherman's 75mm. erupted. At that distance, the tank gunner couldn't miss. The 88 disappeared in a violent ball of red flame. In the turret they ducked, and heard the metal shards slam against the steel.

The Sherman swung round the bend. Frightened young soldiers were huddled behind a makeshift barrier of carts and wine barrels. At 30 m.p.h. *Harvard Crimson* smashed into the barrier. The Sherman rocked violently, but didn't overturn. Next instant it was through, grinding the defenders to red pulp. A head, complete with grey peaked cap and long flying blond hair, sailed in front of van Horn.

He gulped, and besides him Big Red grinned, 'It's sure rough at point, ain't it, Lootenant?' he commented cheerfully, and squirted a stream of brown tobacco juice over the side of the turret.

A minute later the column had disappeared into the night. They were through the 'thin crust'. There was nothing between them and the River Meuse now.

The message had come through thirty minutes before. An excited young voice had broken radio silence to report metallically, 'Harvard, I got 'em! By sheer fluke. They're motoring up the main highway to Huy. There's a whole bunch of Krauts on the road. Jeez, don't I just wish I was a fighter-bomber jock! Best target I've seen since the Falaise Pocket. OK, main Huy highway. Over, Harvard.'

'Roger and out,' van Horn had responded excitedly and had immediately changed the direction of his advance. Mile after mile, hour after hour, the lone armoured column had pushed eastwards, occasionally meeting scattered German resistance, but carrying all in front of them. And now they were on the Meuse.

Standing upright in the turret of *Harvard Crimson*, van Horn surveyed the opposite bank. To his front, the poplars stood up against the dirty white of the false dawn like the teeth of an upturned rake. But the bank was otherwise empty. The Belgian peasants who farmed the other side had fled and if there were any Germans dug in on the heights beyond, they were well-hidden. Nothing stirred up there.

He swung round and focussed his night glasses on the bridge. A couple of the now familiar coal-scuttle helmets slid into the centre of the calibrated glasses. They were sentries on the far end. 'Bridge still occupied,' he whispered to a silently chewing Big Red.

The sergeant shifted his permanent wad of chewing tobacco to his other cheek. 'Yeah, Lootenant, they'll hold it till the rest of their guys are across and then they'll blow it as soon as our boys make an appearance.' He squirted a stream of tobacco juice over the side. 'Sure is a shame, I'd like to get me a bridge. It'd mean a medal, promotion and a chance to get at all that Frog tail waiting on me in Gay Paree.'

Van Horn grinned. Big Red was Regular Army and just like the rest of them. West Pointers or not, that was all they lived for – medals, promotion and tail, in that order.

'I'll talk to the colonel about it,' he said and swung his glasses round to look at the highway leading up to the bridge.

'All the Old Man'll do is to gimme a tough-shit pass to see the chaplain,' Big Red said grumpily. 'That guy don't even know the goddam *word*, leave.'

Van Horn was no longer listening. Biting his lip thoughtfully, he was studying the terrain. He'd have to find a place where whatever came in front of these Wotan killers would not spot his men. And once he had dealt with them, he'd have to be able to roll westwards again swiftly. He didn't have the muscle to tackle what was probably all that was left of the German army, coming down the highway.

Big Red, the veteran, seemed able to read his mind. 'The way I see it, Lootenant,' he said slowly, moving his wad mechanically from one side of his freckled face to the other, 'we've got to be able to zap them and move out kinda swift. 'Cos if we don't, we're gonna get ourselves clobbered, but for sure.'

'Yes, I agree, Red. So?'

'So . . .' Big Red spat once more. Below, the track twanged metallically under the impact. Van Horn waited impatiently. The big Texan NCO liked to take his time. 'Well, I figure we're safest on this side of the highway. We can hit them and bug out for that wood yonder before they know what's hit 'em.'

'Yes, but what about that steep embankment on the other side of the highway? It offers pretty good protection.'

'No one in his right mind, Lootenant,' Red drawled, 'would try to take that gradient with a deuce-and-a-half truck. Shit, the truck's goddam wheels'd fall off under the strain, if the driver didn't get himself plumb killed.'

'Go into hull-down here, you suggest, then?' van Horn persisted.

'Sactly, Lootenant. We line up along the road – here. When they come in sight, we blast them. They'll be easy meat, silhouetted up there on the highway, with no way to go 'cept into the sky.' He spat yet again. Below, the grass turned yellow suddenly. 'Shucks, Lootenant, we're gonna have us a real old Texas-style turkey shoot,' he drawled happily. 'Yessir!'

'I only hope you're right, Red,' van Horn said, suddenly uneasy, as if he half anticipated what was to come . . .

THIRTEEN

Dawn came reluctantly. It was as if the sun did not want to see the war-torn land below yet again. But gradually it started to peep over the stark landscape. Brown, fresh shell-holes, like the work of gigantic moles; the trees, stripped of their branches, like outsize toothpicks; a burnt-out truck, its dead driver sprawled over the smashed wheel; a Tiger, out of fuel and abandoned by its crew; a headless body, the head, still clad in a helmet with a pipe clenched between gritted teeth, a metre away.

Matz, driving the second truck with Schulze, yawned wearily and took his eyes off the leading two-and-a-half tonner, still driven by Washington, covered by a young trooper. 'Great balls of shit,' he groaned, 'ain't we there yet? My tonsils is floating for want of a piss and my arse feels like the look on your ugly mug.'

'Whatever that is supposed to mean, apeturd, I do not know,' Schulze said with assumed dignity, and pulled out his 'flatman'. 'But I do expect you to have a bit of respect for a senior NCO of the Armed SS.' He drank deeply of the spirits and belched pleasurably.

'*Prost!*' Matz toasted him hopefully, his eyes fixed greedily on the bottle in the driving mirror.

'*Prost* – my ass!' Schulze said. 'Yer not supposed to drink and drive, yer know.'

'My throat's like the floor of a parrot's cage,' Matz said pleadingly. 'A gorilla's armpit is moist in comparison with my mouth.'

Schulze relented. He shoved the flatman at his companion. 'All right, but don't go slugging it down like mother's milk. We've got a bit of way to go to the Meuse, and I'll need the rest for breakfast.'

Matz took the bottle greedily with his free hand, neatly swung round a dead cow littering the road, and downed a stiff drink of the plum schnapps. 'Now that's what I call a drink,' he breathed happily. 'My tonsils are beginning to ring like the bells of Spandau Garrison Church.'

'Ay,' Schulze said dourly, and relapsing into silence, started to search the flat Belgian countryside for the first sign of the bridge. They had been travelling all night now, fighting their way through the thousands of fleeing men and vehicles in a desperate attempt to reach the bridge at Huy and safety, before the engineers blew it or the Allied *Jabos* jumped them. At the most they had another hour before the enemy dawn patrol would spot them.

For a moment he studied the convoy – the truck with the girls in front, and behind at a regulation convoy distance, Colonel von Dodenburg, driving the third truck himself. All three of them bore the captured American recognition panels draped over their bonnets and the look-out behind the cab at the .50 calibre anti-aircraft m.g. wore an American helmet and combat jacket. It was the CO's idea. He thought it might fool the Ami *Jabos* if they came down low enough to check the trucks out. Schulze pursed his thick cracked lips doubtfully. Back in the Ami lines they'd know about the hijacked trucks now – and besides, what would American vehicles be doing among the retreating German forces?

Schulze stared at the smashed and splintered trees, the

craters with the dried sterile earth and blackened edges which covered the fields like the scabs of some ugly disease, and shuddered.

'What's up?' Matz asked, eyes fixed on the leading truck.

'Louse ran over my liver.'

'Then kill the bugger,' Matz said routinely.

Schulze said nothing. Instinctively his hand clutched the Schmeisser more tightly. There was an ominous feel about the morning. He knew something was going to happen. They rolled on towards the Meuse.

'Did I ever tell ya the one about the Nigra troop-train that pulled into some little Southern station or other,' one of van Horn's rednecks was saying thickly, 'and all the local high yaller gals sashéed up to meet it . . .'

Next to him, Big Red was whistling *The Yellow Rose of Texas* tunelessly through his dingy front teeth. Moodily, van Horn stared at the landscape of death – the gigantic rubbish-dump of burnt, twisted metal and human flesh, and asked himself once again what made human beings do things like this to each other. Four years at Harvard had certainly not prepared him for man's inhumanity to man: that underneath the forest of upturned rifles stuck into the ground by their bayonets, there was a man who wore a different uniform, and had been killed because of it; and that the putrid, black paste on the wall of the tank yonder was what was left of a man who had been alive only twenty-four hours before. He took his gaze away from the dead German sprawled out, hands outstretched as if on a cross, staring at him accusingly, and tried to force himself to listen to the redneck. Perhaps he was just too sensitive for combat.

'So the high yaller gals met the looey in charge of the train, a white guy, and they ask him, kinda innocent-like, what type of sojers he's got aboard, and the white looey sez, "Well, lady I've got some coloured privates . . ." Now wait for it, guys. To which the high yaller gal sez,' the redneck simpered in a high-pitched imitation of what he

163

supposed was a typical Negress's voice, ' *"Lor, Mr Looten-ant, sir, ain't you the fancy one!"* '

There was a rumble of low laughter from the others and van Horn smiled. The joke wasn't too bad after all; it made a change after the usual stuff about the sexual prowess of 'buck niggers', as his men always called black men. All the same, it still showed the usual prejudice. He sighed, realizing just how much of a gulf separated him from his men.

'*Lootenant!*' the lazy tone had gone from Big Red's voice. Abruptly his face was keen, alert. 'Can you hear 'em?'

'Hear what?'

'Them!'

Lieutenant van Horn, the Third, cocked his head to one side in order to hear better. For a moment he heard nothing. Then it was there. The soft hum of engines far away to the West. 'Do you think—?' The question died on his lips. Three dark low shapes had breasted the rise, and van Horn knew instinctively that the two-and-a-half ton trucks could only be those that they were waiting for. SS Assault Regiment Wotan had arrived on the scene. The time had come to do battle. Licking suddenly dry lips, he cried, 'All right, fellers, this is it. *Here they come!*'

The sky was a pale-orange now. The morning was completely still. The poplars which lined the raised highway were motionless. No wind stirred their bomb-shattered branches. On the horizon, the Meuse shimmered in the first sunlight. An air of heavy, tense expectancy hung over the whole area.

Matz did not seem to notice. Effortlessly steering the big truck loaded with sleeping troopers, he sang the same old refrain, over and over again. '*My parrot don't eat hard-boiled eggs. But he's crazy about caviare and gherkins.*'

In the end, it was too much for Schulze, who was trying to doze beside him. Opening his eyes, he glared at the wizened-faced driver and bellowed, 'Cut it out, you ringing fairy. We're right in the shit and you sing that crap. What are you, you garden dwarf, some kind of sadist, eh?'

'Can't allus look at the gloomy side of things,' Matz commented. 'Once we're across that bridge, and billetted somewhere, I'm gonna cut myself off a piece of that blonde's ass, or my name ain't Matz.'

'What on, pigeon-prick?' Schulze said contemptuously. 'A piece of dry maize bread and a sip of water? That sort of grub don't put much ink in yer fountain pen, even for a handsome feller like mesen who is naturally highly sexed.'

Matz shrugged and neatly skirted a bomb-crater. 'Hungry or full, it don't matter when yer in luv. It goes . . . it goes.' He steered the truck within a millimetre of the drop to the right in order to avoid a dead cow.

'You'll go, too – for a hop, Matzi, if you pull damnfool tricks like that again,' Schulze breathed, hanging on to the seat as he stared down at the three-metre drop to the fields. 'Watch the sodding road. You nearly had us over then.'

'No sweat, Sch—'

His words were drowned by the first crash of the Sherman's 75mms. In front of them the truck carrying the women was struck. Its axle collapsed. Screaming, burning women were flung to the ground. The unknown attackers fired again. The truck was lifted clean into the air, shaking out dead and dying whores, arms and legs whirling crazily, a mad mess of bodies and flame. Like panic-stricken rabbits surprised in a field of summer wheat by the harvesters, the ones who were still alive ran straight into the chattering machine-guns to be scythed down relentlessly. The ambush had commenced.

'Oh my God, *women!*' Lt van Horn cried in horror, as the last of the whores was mown down, her arms raised to the unfeeling sky piteously, as if in supplication. '*Cease fire* . . . For Heaven's sake, *cease fire!*'

'*Are you nuts?*' a sweating Red yelled at his side. 'Those bastards are gonna get away—' He grabbed for the intercom.

Van Horn fended him off with his free hand. 'To all

165

units,' he bellowed over the mike. 'Cease fire! Do you hear? Cease fire! *Now!* That's an order!'

Before Big Red had time to interrupt, he snapped, 'Driver – driver, advance . . . To all units – follow me onto the road!'

Churning up mud, *Harvard Crimson* started to move towards where the two remaining trucks had skidded to a surprised stop behind the burning deuce-and-a-half.

Big Red shook his head and spat over the side contemptuously. 'You'll be sorry,' he said.

What happened next was to prove the big Texan to be right.

Abruptly, the first Ami tank broke through the thick milky-white smoke pouring from the shattered truck. *'Now!'* von Dodenburg commanded urgently. The two troopers ran forward, weighed down by the full jerricans. Big Red swung the m.g. on the turret round. He pressed the trigger. The leading trooper went down with a scream. The Sherman rolled over him. The other German swung the contents of the can in a great stream at the tank's metal side, just as it ran over him, churning his young body to bloody pulp.

'Oh, my Christ,' Big Red screamed in sudden fear as he realized what the Krauts were up to. 'Driver—'

Too late. The Kraut officer standing in the direct path of the Sherman fired the bell-shaped pistol he held in his hand. A soft plop and the Very flare exploded directly on the Sherman's petrol-soaked armour-plates.

'Flame!' van Horn screamed in horror, realizing too late how the Germans had tricked them, as the blue greedy flames engulfed the Sherman, hissing into the compartments, blinding the gunner, sending him back crying in agony, eyeballs charred and obscene, hushing into the turret consuming everything with their dreadful searing fire. Big Red made one last effort to spit and then the blue flames wreathed him, turning him into a frantically writhing horror. Van Horn flung up his arms to protect his face. To no

166

avail. In an instant his hands were charred claws through which the bones gleamed a bright white. Blinded instantly, howling with terrible pain, he tried to clamber out, but was unable to do so, and fell back weakly, half hanging out of the turret, letting the terrible red monster devour him in its fiery maw.

A second later, the shells in the Sherman's ready locker exploded. The Sherman's ten-ton turret sailed high into the air, carrying the black pygmies which had been Big Red, the product of Texas share-croppers and the Depression, and Lieutenant Clarence van Horn, the Third, scion of Boston Brahmins and Harvard, with it. *Harvard Crimson* disappeared.

'*Start up . . . Down the embankment!*' Von Dodenburg cried desperately above the rattle of the advancing Shermans and the fresh burst of fire.

Matz swung the wheel round. '*Jesus, Mary, Joseph!*' Schulze yelled in fear. Matz didn't hesitate. First gear roaring, he edged the big truck over the dip. Schulze closed his eyes. Behind, the troopers held on to the metal stanchions with one hand, firing their weapons at the advancing Americans with the other. The truck's left wheel hit a hidden rock. Instinctively the little corporal, crouched over the wheel, his face lathered with sweat, hit the brakes. The truck swerved to the right. For one horrible instant it seemed as if it would overturn. Schulze prayed fervently. Somehow Matz managed to retain control with hands that were wet with sweat. The truck screamed with the strain. Every stanchion howled metallically. Gravel and mud streamed up in a blinding flurry behind its racing wheels. Matz felt his stomach floating high above his head. He relaxed the pressure on the brake. The truck shot forward. It hit the bottom hard. Behind, the troopers were flung to the floor.

Schulze swallowed the bitter bile which threatened to choke him and opened his eyes, in the same moment that Matz hit the accelerator. 'Holy straw-sack, Matzi,' he said thickly, 'you're a shitting automobile artist!' Then he aimed his Schmeisser out of the window and fired a burst at the surprised Amis, sweeping a whole bunch of them off the deck of one of the Shermans, as if they were flies. Behind them von Dodenburg's truck commenced the descent.

They hit the American armour at thirty kilometres an hour. Like pirates boarding fat, startled prizes, the troopers dropped from the two trucks onto the Shermans' decks. Von Dodenburg smashed the butt of his pistol onto a tank commander's head. In spite of his leather helmet, the man's skull caved in. He fell to the floor, dragging the wires of the intercom behind him in blood-stained confusion. At von Dodenburg's back, his self-appointed bodyguard fired a murderous burst into the tank's interior. Completely out of control, the driver dead at his wheel, but his foot clamped down on the accelerator, the Sherman began to go round in a circle.

'Come on, sir,' Schulze yelled, laughing uproariously. 'Let's get off. Round-abouts allus make me dizzy.' He dropped lightly over the side, followed by his CO. Next instant a burst of enemy fire shattered the Schmeisser he held in his big paw. He stared down at what was left of the smoking metal in disgust. 'Great crap on the Christmas Tree,' he cried, 'I suppose they'll expect me to champ the Amis to death with my choppers now! The things I do for Führer, Folk and Fatherland.' Effortlessly, he swung himself on the deck of the next Sherman and began the business of bloody slaughter once more.

For the next five minutes, no quarter was given or expected. Murder, mayhem and massacre reigned. Razor-sharp metal sliced into soft flesh. Bone splintered. Blood spattered the decks of the Shermans in great ugly red gobs. Blood-tinged bubbles of saliva frothed on the mouths of dying tankers. Eerie inhuman screams surged up from deep within them. But the crazed young men of Wotan, all their pent-up fury at the horror of the long retreat released at last, showed no mercy. Hacking, slicing, slitting, chopping, stabbing, they cut through the stalled, surprised Americans, screaming with blood-lust, filled with the old atavistic desire to slaughter. And then what was left of them were running, uniforms ripped and stained with fresh blood, wildly for the river, throwing away their weapons in their haste, leaving behind them the massacred point of the 37th U.S. Tank Battalion.

Swimmers and non-swimmers alike, they rushed into the Meuse. The cold water hit them with a shock. In a flash they were floundering in its depths, striking out as best they could towards the waving figures in field-grey who were already beginning to wade in on the other side to help them. They had done it. *The long retreat was over . . .*

FOR FOLK, FATHERLAND AND FÜHRER

As always before an attack, dawn came with maddening slowness. Colonel von Dodenburg, crouched in the command bunker, wondered whether it was really coming at all, or whether his eyes had just become accustomed to the darkness. His whole body ached, and he wondered just how long it would be before he dared light a cigarette and savour the blessed smoke.

Now it had stopped drizzling, and here and there men were clambering out of their foxholes in the September gloom to urinate against the sides of the concrete bunkers. Colonel von Dodenburg stared at their dark outlines next to those of the massive pillboxes and wondered, when the real attack on the Reich started, whether the concrete line which stretched from Holland to Switzerland could really stop them. The Atlantic Wall[1] hadn't stopped the Allies, nor the Seine Line. As for the line of the Meuse, they had been forced to abandon it within a week. Now, only a handful of metres away this grey September morning, the point of the U.S. 1st Army was preparing to attack into Germany itself.

He folded his damp blanket and lit his first cigarette of the day, coughing harshly as the smoke bit deep into his lungs. Around him, his 'staff', Schulze and Matz, two 17-year-old lieutenants and the fat-bellied Golden Pheasant[2] Katzer, the National Socialist Party Officer,[3] started to stir uneasily.

Like all the rest of his hastily flung-together battle group,

[1] The fortifications along the French coast.
[2] Contemptuous name for Nazi Party officials, due to the amount of gold braid they affected.
[3] Party Commissars attached to fighting units to engender National Socialist spirit among the troops.

which presently masqueraded under the proud name of Wotan, they looked ashen, dirty, unshaven and depressed. For a moment, Colonel von Dodenburg remembered the Regiment he had led into battle in Normandy a mere three months before, the veterans of Italy, tough, bronzed, confident, their chests heavy with 'tin', leading the eager, well-trained volunteers of the Hitler Youth – the élite of the élite – and sudden tears flooded his eyes. They were all gone, vanished as if they had never even existed. And for what? 'For what?' he whispered to himself, and with a soft groan clambered out of the damp hole.

Now the barrage which would soften up the Amis before they attacked began to hiss over their heads. The men didn't seem to notice; they were too apathetic. They crouched in the wet grass and stared numbly into nothing. Most of them were strangers to one another as it was, impressed into the SS from the Air Force or Navy, or culled from the hospitals or rear-line units; they didn't even talk to each other. Wearily von Dodenburg walked through their ranks, patting a forlorn soldier on the shoulder here, smiling encouragingly there, exchanging a few cheery words with others, but there was no response from them. They were sunk in deep gloom, knowing now, in this September of the year 1944, that there was nothing to look forward to, except death.

Sadly, despondently, von Dodenburg walked back to his command bunker. Schulze was rubbing big wet feet that hadn't been dry for a week, while Matz was attempting to fry a sausage on the end of a bayonet over a miserable fire of wet woods that stubbornly refused to burn.

'She was a nice slit,' Schulze was saying wearily. 'Gonna open a hotel on the Rhine. That Rosie was just my collar-size.'

'Poor bitch,' Matz agreed without enthusiasm. 'All those years working on her back, getting that red rim – and never lived to see the fruits of her labours. Poor slit – all of 'em poor slits.'

'Yer,' Schulze agreed. 'It's allus the same – it's the rich

what has the pleasure and the poor what takes the blame. I mean,' he went on, sudden iron in his voice, as the thunder of the guns grew ever louder, 'what the shitting hell is this caper about? The Ivans are on the Oder, the Amis are in spitting distance over yonder and we're supposed to defend the Reich with a bunch of broken-down rear-echelon stallions, cripples and pansy sea-lions! The enemy's in our backyard, trying to get his dirty mitts up *frauchen*'s[1] skirt, and we still think we can win. They mustn't have all their cups in their cupboard up there in Berlin.' He glowered angrily at his big dirty feet, from which the skin hung in damp strips. 'Arseholes!'

Slowly and dramatically, the Party Officer rose to his feet, his fat belly thrust out importantly, his tunic unadorned save with the War Service cross, Third Class. 'Sergeant-Major,' he said severely, selecting his words with care, 'what you have just said is treachery, one hundred percent treachery to the Führer and our folk comrades. Our Führer, Adolf Hitler,' he said the words as if they were in quotation marks, 'in his infinite wisdom knows we will still win through to final victory because he has many secrets up his sleeve. There are secrets – but I mustn't talk about those. Believe me, we have terrible new weapons that will make the Russians and the Anglo-Saxons plead with us for mercy. All our Führer demands of us is that we believe. *For Folk, Fatherland and Führer, we march on to final victory!* Are they not stirring words, Sergeant-Major?'

Matz's reaction was to raise his left cheek and fart. Schulze wiped the pearl of snot from his pinched, red nose contemptuously. 'Folk, Fatherland and Führer, my ass,' he growled. 'Germany's finished, finee, kaputt. We've had it, lardguts!'

'What—'

Von Dodenburg glared down at the men in the pit and cried, 'Be silent, *all of you!*'

'What do you know of war, Captain,' he addressed the Party Officer, 'that you can talk to front-line swine like us

[1] Roughly, 'little woman'.

173

in that manner? You haven't seen comrade after comrade killed or maimed in battles which have grown more desperate and one-sided as the years have passed by.' He glared at the suddenly deflated fat officer. 'Do you know how many times this Regiment has been re-created since 1939? I shall tell you. One dozen times! Can you imagine how many good men have died in its ranks in that time for other things than just a silly motto dreamed up in the Ministry of Propaganda? SS Assault Regiment Wotan fights for other values.'

As the roar of the many shells screaming over their heads grew in intensity like that of some trapped infuriated beast, a tremendous rage overcame Colonel von Dodenburg. He flashed a burning look at the grey, war-worn faces all around him and felt for them – the impossible demands the war made upon them, their suffering, the final sacrifice that so many of them would be called upon to make in a few months. Haggard face flushed with rage, he brandished his pistol like a crazy man and cried, '*Well, you dogs of death . . . What are you waiting for? . . . Do you want to live for ever?*'

Not even looking to see if they were following him, Colonel von Dodenburg raced forward into the deafening thunder of the new battle.

His men hesitated for only a fraction of a second. Then, carried away suddenly by the madness of war, they streamed after him, screaming crazily.

In an instant, the burning gloom of battle had swallowed them up and they vanished into history, leaving behind them only the eerie echo of that last desperate cry which seemed to go on for ever. '*Dogs of death . . . do you want to live for ever . . .?*'

SEALION

Richard Cox

The German Paratroops jumped at dawn as they had done in Holland, in Belgium, in Norway. But this time there were more of them . . . the time was six o'clock on the morning of September 22, 1940 . . . by breakfast time close on 90,000 troops were successfully ashore on the beaches between Folkestone and Seaford.

OPERATION SEALION: the German invasion of England. Minutely planned. What would have happened if the invasion had gone ahead as planned?

Hitler had intended to capture the whole of Southern England within only ten days. Sealion is a vivid, authentic documentary novel based on a War Game organized by the Royal Military Academy, Sandhurst, umpired by six top British and German officers in an effort to determine whether Hitler would have succeeded.

SEALION is the thrilling story of the first invasion of Britain since 1066.

MAXIMUM EFFORT

James Campbell

The High-tension, fast moving novel of a Bomber
Squadron savagely mauled in the great saturation raids
on Germany. In an atmosphere charged with the
tautness of a bomb-aimer's flak-lit compartment the
lives, loves and fears of the men who manned the
Halifaxes of Bomber Command are vividly, even brutally,
portrayed.

This is bomber warfare stripped of its glamour;
warfare powerfully, yet authentically set against the
background of the massive thousand-bomber attacks
on Hitler's Third Reich. The fury of those night skies of
early 1944 flames through the drama of men keyed to
breaking point; men whose life-span was measured in
days, sometimes in hours.